Table of Contents

LIEBER

Early Life and Context

1988 - 2002

Michael Lieber was born Michael John Griffiths on the 6th of May 1988 in Birmingham, England; Soon after, his parents divorced, resulting in him, his Mother and three siblings relocating to the South of Wales, where they settled in a prosperous port town called Tenby. Lieber's creative nature manifested at this time in the form of magic, and could be found busking around the port from the age of ten; together with his messy hair, he wore a traditional blue suit that was remarked to be two sizes too big for him. Despite his many talents, Lieber as a child remained completely illiterate even as he approached his 11th birthday, it was by order of his Father in 1998 that he was moved back to England on his own, to attend schooling at the Maple Hayes Dyslexia Institute in Lichfield (now known as the Maple Hayes School for Dyslexics), the Institute resided within an old stately manor on top of a hill, behind gated security and was run by its founders Dr. Neville Brown and Dr. Daryl Brown who were pioneering a new and controversial teaching technique called 'The Morpheme Method'; the method required the subject to memories hundreds of symbols, each one representing a different segment of every single word in the English language. Lieber was one of ten children involved in the study. Although resistant and homesick at first, it was a chance conversation with the two doctors that sparked a change within him, stating that if he didn't learn to write, all the stories he had in his head would die with him and be lost forever; after this, he committed to the method entirely, the result of which was a remarkable outcome, his illiteracy shrank away with every symbol he memorised, mastering Shakespeare's iambic pentameter in a matter of hours; soon he was reading through countless books in the institute's private library, and eventually began to write his own simple works. Although most of his writings from this period were either lost or destroyed, one narrative poem survives; 'Elle's Logic', which he later adapted into one of his novellas (The Boy And The Goldlock). During his five years at the Institute, he was deemed in one scientific study, to be 'a child prodigy of the Morpheme Method', and to this day, Lieber remains one of the best case studies for its validity.

2003 - 2022

Upon leaving the institute at fifteen, Lieber found himself at a loss, until a stage manager and friend of the family, suggested he be placed in a production of Oliver Twist that was being staged at the Garrick Theatre in the summer months of 2003. Lieber agreed, and filled in for one of the workhouse boys; before long, he became enchanted by the theatre and adored the flamboyant company of actors; this led to a brief enrolment at The Oxford School Of Speech And Drama, but he soon dropped out after six months, declaring "Drama schools seek to destroy any and all natural talent", before moving to London in 2008 to make his name as a playwright and actor. He would spend a total of seven years in London studying the plays of Oscar Wilde and began work on a three-act farce entitled 'Conning the Vales'. In 2011, he witnessed the burning down of the Tandem Centre during the London Riots and help defend The Royal Standard pub in Colliers Wood from looters and petrol bombs; he also starred in a number of films throughout this period, including the award winning period drama Ramanujan in 2014, and the psychological thriller A Room To Die For produced by Sony Pictures in 2017. During a production of Salome at the Courtyard Theatre, he fell madly in love with a young actress named Atlanta Johnson; for reasons unknown, the two separated, although it is speculated that his dwindling funds made London living unaffordable; the concept of wealth and social class would be a regular theme in his work to come. Heartbroken, he returned to the only place that felt remotely like home, the city of Lichfield, he began drinking heavily, grew a large beard and desperate to forget not only Atlanta but the London theatre, he rewrote his unperformed stage play into prose and renamed it The War Hero; this low point in his life transformed what was once a light-hearted farce into undoubtedly the darkest and most philosophical novel he ever wrote. Upon writing his second and third works of prose, The Boy And The Goldlock and Helga Dune, he began to see the romantic themes of his work and how they lined up perfectly with the stylings of nineteenth-century literature, and proposed to join the likes of Donna Tartt in defining the importance of neo-romanticism in the 21st century.

THE
WAR
HERO

A NOVEL

LARKWELL

Dedication

Dedicated to Dr. Daryl Brown and
Dr. Neville Brown of

Maple Hayes Hall *'Thank you for the Icons'*

The Voice of Creation

The greatest redemption is between the war of two evils, their very retaliation reveals their goodly nature, but this as a statement does not apply to you, not you my dovely darlings, my P and V of perfect porcelain, simple to the ear but true nonetheless, boys will be boys and girls will be girls, in short, you can do no wrong in my eyes, if I had any of course.

I remember, everything, but to be specific the day you were born, all tiny tips and terrible tantrums you were, dancing a careless phantasm that I still often envy, the adolescent sulk of blissful melancholy, your first kiss and the pressure of profession everlasting,... you cursed me then once; and then again in your middle-aged load bearing weight of servility, a father, mother, martyr and lover; and alas my jaded doves, that graceful flight of old, the waddling decade of crimson velvet, coupled with an overwhelming wave of technology that appears so frightening to the plagued brain of cherry picked nostalgia, shrinking ever shrinking to that inevitable blue-veined serpented limb, out stretched to a cracked ceiling, mutely crying my harrowing name, praying and pleading for one last adventure.

So many lives, I'm cursed more times than I ever could bear, but please, please realise, that even in your last fragile moments, I will forever be your gentle svelte with rosy cheeks as you are, were and always shall be my little ones, and although I may grow brutal and hydeish, my attention turned by tender tadpoles of light, I will never forget you, I can't forget you, which is why I so want you to understand me, after all I understand 'you', at least I think I have that capacity; and as a consequence I have only just now realised how god awfully depressing I've just been.

So let us raise ourselves Comrades! let us open our gullets and pour warm liquid chocolate down till we glow bright with its wild warmth, let us breathe fully into our eager lungs and admire the view however bleak it may seem, for this journey is not for the weak, it is for the painted braves, the worse of the willing and can be found In the reluctant sleeping brain of a freshly trenched and now newly bedded boy soldier of barely eligible age as far as death is concerned, but to my dis-embodied throbbings, this predicament is quite matter of fact, he lays under a canvas canopy, between khaki coloured sheets, he's labelled a soldier, he's got himself hurt hence the dying, simple yet effective. Try to ignore the pungent stench of broken bravery and the soft blistered shuffles of sweaty teenage nurses. Ignore the rouge innards of this ever engulfing tent and the brown stringed elegant erection that spars so enthusias-tically with the rattling French winds; gather round him close my pea-sized patriots, closer still to his pitifully perturbed eyelids, there's no need to be respectful, for this sad claustrophobic moment in a mad man's memory is to be used in such general terms as an earwig doorway and nothing more.

So shrink to match and join me with a smile, we'll march past his ear drum.

Stomp, stomp, stomp, Company halt! Let us dig through the fear and advance over this neatly knotted compendium, help me lift this early onset of carnal capillaries. I can feel us getting deeper, it's a long while since anyone has been this far, you better mind your step or the kid might wake up.

If you look to your left, you will see that even in his formative years he has some very enthusiastic yet highly controversial views in regards to love, loss and pain and although this is not uncommon in penniless, post Victorian sprogs, it will be considered by future origins as a rather nasty shade of cruel and or malicious, and if you look straight ahead, how wonderful, there it is, just what I was looking for, It maybe small and hard to find but here it is nonetheless, that homely mirage that can be found in any developed brain if you track back this far, their home, your home, whatever form it may take.

For this shrapnel loving, hot fevered Tommy boy, It lays in a blackened streak of perfect aim which although frequently used, is often regarded by the rest of its colourful palette as all black eyes, black smoke and indeed black industrial country, conveniently centralised in middle England.

To some, this canal-mild metropolis may not be the most exotic of locations, entranced with evil dwarfs and fairy kingdoms, but for him, a lovely messy nest and far, far, away from the bullying bullets and half buried boredom. The delicious monkey bait I hope to entice you with though, is not so much our landing spot but rather the time period. You see the Kaiser's in the dirt and Mr. Nazi-gas-man is still sending messages, the celebrating is over and its business as usual, the usual being haze and shadow to the average consumer, pillared between two towering bookends of tearful playground tyranny.

The year is 1925, May 8th, Birmingham city centre, Staffordshire, England, landing coordinates 52.4862° North and 1.8904° West respectively.

Well go on then, I expect you to jump in, or rather down, falling down, full with me my warrior women and men of iron, through the atmosphere of empty clouds and passing pigeons, let the sub-zero elements fling back your arms and embrace every fearsome flap of your shuddering clothes as we plummet down, down increasingly down. You there! No need to scream, we'll float before we hit the firmness of the Earth I promise you that.

Right class, I want to see nicely pointed tippy toes, passing the lamp lights and softly land foot by foot firmly on the ground and pirouette, plié, plié and finish with a flair, is everyone accounted for?...good! Now we can begin.

Chapter One:

Mr. Lidman

Despite the menacing Midlands chill nipping at every passing nape, Mr. Sun tries with high determination to beat down bright upon the cobble damp streets, the early morning sounds sporadically piercing the dewy, new day silence like a broken wind chime, each prominent bong belonging to the usual goblinesque creatures that limp about at 7.30am on a Friday morning, with one particular relevant ruckus spearing above all others and puzzling pie-eyed pedestrians. The heavy repetition of weary running, its echo-echo fading with every quick footed connection as a young puppy-fatted male's flustered panicky pins, carry him panting around the corner of a locked and local library.

Avoiding a near collision with a doddering old dear with a barking corgi, the youthful yet exhausted figure accelerates once more down the Birmingham high street, his worried expression, a red tomato, whistling overheated jets of propelled vapour into the cold morning mist.

Checking his watch in a flailing flap, he dashes the bag-eyed gaze of a yawning market stall, its newly read newspapers scream at his running rush with their big bold fonts 'Easterly winds are coming! Storm Tonight!'

Slowing down at the bare belated time of 7.37am, chubby and late skids to a halt outside a gold-like building, styled in Neo Palladian sand stone, three story's tall with its sobering title nestled between a similar number of grumpy granite eagles, perched proudly around the deeply engraved lintel letters 'Lidman & Son Accountancy Est. 1856'.

Bounding three steps at a time, while simultaneously trying to improve his overall appearance, paying due attention to a newly discovered jam stain between tie and shirt, proceeded by an act of clumsiness, a clowning trip at the last step, landing at the base of the door with a thud. Regaining his winded self in a manner that only a robust toddler would attempt, he plants and then vertically extends both legs before craning up the rest of his upper blubber. Ignoring the shallow injuries to his roly-poly ham of a left arm and right hand, seeing them as a passing trifle compared to the terrible tempest that awaits him inside. Painfully pulling, parting and entering past the oversized baton brass handles, he intakes a profound lingering musk of ink covered copper and chemicalized floor cleaner, which to the fresh aired nostril translates to an unnatural sweetness upon entry.

A large, unevolved, hollowed out hall of a business, swallows up his slovenly silhouette, complete with complimentary ear plugs, wall to wall hat racks and seven high reaching windows on either side, stretching their ambitious altitude to a granular ceiling, its adjacent floor infested by row after row of individually seated, silently suited

Accountants typing as vigorously as their digits will allow. The repetitive and almost deafening sound of click-clack-click of fifty or more, heavy adding machines being prodded beyond their warranty, reverberates around the sparsely covered, wood panelled walls.

Leading from the entrance, through the chaos, an eight-foot wide empty aisle of mottled brown, protracts its long length to an intimidating grandeur staircase. Peeping weaves revealing its once youthful shade of emerald green.

Still wheezing slightly from the fall, the not so punctual porkster spy's his empty desk laying lonely at the back of the room, next to a drafty cracked window pane and a wall leaning step ladder. Creeping stealthily through the sea of bowed heads and billowing paper ribbons, his greasy comb-over colleagues glance up at him one by one with a chased look of amusement and glee before melting back down to a deep rooted absorption.

Reaching the untidy work station, he channels the fine physicality of one who arrived at seven o'clock sharp with half an hours beavering boxed up and ready to go. Slicking a dirty bowl-cut with a gob of spit, he tugs at a stubborn desk drawer to release a congealed fountain pen, but before the pussy pink hue of his bubble-fish cheeks can return to their natural shade of pasty white, smack! A bony opened hand strikes the back of his head with such force he buckles forward like a poorly stuffed rag doll onto the messy ink splattered work surface. Recoiling back with a bulbous bolt of stinging pain, covering temple and crown with wheedling digits, the dilated dots of an unlucky man wince up at a tall, elongated frame with two immaculately clean spectacle lenses glinting back at him.

"Late again Codbery! Dear, dear, oh dear" barked the tall man with a few dry tuts added on the end.

"It was the bed-clock Mr. Richmore sir, didn't ding its bells, It won't happen again, promise it won't"

"Promise! It's past your scheduled time of employment, warned you before, made a real point of it too."

"Sir I'm begging you I am, don't tell Mr. Lidman! I'll do ten times the work I normally do, a hundred times more!" pleaded the Cod in a panting panic.

"..I'm sorry, no more time for you lad, chances a'plenty you've had, now get up them stairs sharpish."

Welling up, Cod blubbers onto the sleeve of his ill fitting, second hand suit, the tall skelly bone standing reaperish with folded shoulder limbs, infected by a toughened glare, contemplating over the raucous sound of click-clack-click whether to grant one last shred of sympathy for Codbery's forth disregard for precise punctuality. Decision quickly made, Richmore angrily tightens his beautifully ironed navy grey tie deep into the drooping folds of loose skin below the chin before lunging forward and roughly hoisting the weeping blotter to a standing blub.

"Listen here our'kid! It's my neck on the chop if he found out, the boot, the big push, the big goodbye, you think I'm willing to risk it, ya'kipping on a cloud you are, head office! Now!.."

In a strained act of kindness, the beanpoled mean man stuffs into Codbery's fat hand a neatly folded white cotton handkerchief from a conservative waistcoat. Mournfully Cod slugs through the field of clicking calculators to the centralised aisle of mottled brown. Swinging a pair of soggy muffin-eyes to an impatient Richmore, pointing a long knobbly finger towards the narrow double doors horribly accessible via the grim grandeur staircase. Proceeding with a dry gullet, the boy ascends the dusty steps, wiping away the streaming snot from under an ink stained sniffer to the added accompaniment of looks and sniggers, his increased elevation revealing a vertical line of white light between the ajar wooden twins dominating a dark spacious landing. Creeping a few feet forward, cloaked in shadow, uncontrollably chomping his jagged fingernails, he performs a leaned peep through the glowing gap to the ominous office beyond. Whizzing left and right, the beady bulb of Cod scans the room of doom, famous among the lower orders for loudly spitting out unemployed meat gristle from its inner enigma, a terrifying spectacle that was increasingly talked about but never actually seen.

Making out the faint outline shape of a sinewy figure hunched heavily over an old oak desk, the narrow double doors snitch to their beloved master with an almighty creak, causing the lumbering lad to leap three-feet back from the mischievous hinges, not moving a muscle for fear of emulation from its brotherly floor boards. His fear willy erected further by a growling gravelly grunt resonating from inside the semi-sealed enclosure.

"What is it now Richmore?..."

Cod says nothing, statued still, bear teeth in shadow. The rumbling room oscillates a second boom.

"It better be good news on this day..."

Overcome with a sudden flightful adrenaline, most likely inspired by the hellish lower floor sounds of Mr. Richmore manhandling yet another ill fated employee, something about wearing red socks and it not even being Christmas, provoking a forward bound with a handle grabbing hand and opening fist, craning his portly oval mug through the gaping gap.

"It's Codbery sir! Milton Codbery, junior clerk and that, sorry for any disturb'in."

The fat boy not looking up in an uneasy slink, quickly plans three pathetic gestures to engage sympathy from an unpeeked employer; the first a raised gaze with the second and third maneuvers being a helpless wry smile before bowing his head shamefully down for a finishing third. The first and second are performed perfectly, Coddy does indeed look up and does indeed give a small wry smile, but the last vital break of connection is instantaneously betrayed and rapidly replaced with a bewitched and bubbered stare as two bright blue, sapphire eyes fix to his own with a profound frown of disturbed peace.

"Yes, I am aware Mr. Codbery, well?" grunted a clement Boss from behind the desk.

The blobby boy tries to articulate from a sandal dry pie-hole, projecting only hot husks of Sahara air.

"...On second, no need," Boss added, dropping an octave lower. "There's only one reason you'd be sent up here, late more than once?"

Wilting with embarrassment, Cod shamefully nods at his uncomfortably small shoes, helpless under the dulcet grumbles, not appearing meek or mild mannered, quite the reverse, the shy bossly sentences made Codbery feel more lowly and dispensable then all the raving Richmond's of his life put together.

"...If it's more than once Mr. Codbery...you'd better take a seat."

Infiltrating the small, rectangular shaped office with its crumbling, germ infested decor and depressingly lit corridor leading off to an eerie darkness, a rickety guest chair greets the grubby Cod, his fishy eye-line falling to a strategically placed desk plaque, the bold New Roman lettering of 'Managing Director - Daniel J Lidman' unpolished and barely made out through the old grooves of grime.

As the old boss licks through a leather bound book of attendance, the late lad reflects over the various, break time rumours he had heard in regards to what the seldom seen 'Lidman' actually looked like. Out of all the over exaggerations,

Codbery had two favourites, the one about him being seven foot tall, four foot wide and living a secret double life along the borders of Mexico, wrestling under the ticket selling pseudonym El'Lido De Mono, followed by the second migrating myth about him being steaming drunk one new year's eve and playfully purchasing, on a whim, a small Buddhist island off the coast of Japan and having it officially renamed Lid-land. Being fairly certain that neither of these statements were true, it added a strange deflated note of surrealism. Here he was, right in front of him, running a cracked fingernail down the C's on page 12, not the mountain man of lower floor legend at all. In fact he was quite small, certainly on the side of broad but yet compacted, as if the years had shrunken his once immense mass, however the origin still remained, impressive he thought, almost mesmerising, his features are striking, a noble nose, large forehead and piercing lunar lagoon eyes suffocated by a sea of long crow's feet, hairy and hunched with an unyielding weight creaking down onto the old oak desk. Cod even contemplated the humorous possibility, that if some near bankrupt zoo in a faraway land, had bizarrely shaved a handful of elderly silverback gorillas in a desperate dash to improve attendance, forgiveness would be given to any for thinking one had cleverly escaped, smuggled itself aboard a cargo ship to fulfill its lifelong dream of running a midlands accountancy firm.

As the hiding page name 'Codbery Milton' finally surrenders with a white calligraphy flag, a cold arctic air blow pearls along Coddy's neck line, the culprit, a double hung window at office end, half open, rattling from the ever changing weather.

"Looks like that storm's dropping in Sir, might be the worse on record in twenty years my Mam said," bumbled the boy, attempting to lighten the sombre setting. "Would you like me to close it...the window Sir? It's awfully chilly..."

Morphing from a studious mute, Lidman sharp barks with such sudden volume his near employee scare jumps as a result.

"Jammed!..needs fix'in, says here you were late...at the beginning of this year, 28th of January, forty-five minutes and you were given a warning."

Boss reclines to a pensive sulk.

"Mr. Codbery, you were employed at this company to be sufficient, not to be spectacular, not to be mediocre, but simply sufficient, and this behaviour lacks a great deal of...sufficiency, wouldn't you agree?"

"Y..y..yes sir" stuttered the boy.

Choked with a leather strap, the late book is tightly rebound and put away by brutish bossery.

"Good time keeping is a must Mr. Codbery...I'm afraid to say, your working relationship with Lidman & Son, will have to regretfully... come to an end."

The deep needlish note pricks the inapt fat lad setting off a sloppy whimper with bungling shirt boobys.

"Oh ple-e-ase! Don't sack me Sir, I love this job, I need this job!..Mam takes me'pay for stews! You like her stew Sir, she bought ya'some last June, big pot of it, remember Sir!.."

Ignoring the Cod soon to be served with chips, a stern DL fondles flat the necessary form and begins filling it in with kinky rough ticks, one box, two box, three box, four box.

Head caught by inky palms, the fatty rocks back and forth, hyperventilating in the rickety guest chair until the final detail remains, a blood red stamp of completion in the low right hand corner.

Lifting a steely stamper from a gungy preparation pad, Lidman acknowledges the Lad's silent wet sob, before aggressively bringing it down with a loud metallic clang so heartbreaking that Cod gives out a tiny whimper at the moment of connection. Head aligned with rattling knees, holding up a young quivering hand to receive his freshly prepared severance sheet, the sharp paper slides between his Darwinian fingers, recoiling it back to survey the official ruby red mark of a bad day as a vast perplexity infects his eggshell shade. The stamp overlapping the square, not of a nightmarish red nor does it say completed, instead a still glistening, circular blue stamp has taken its place, stating that this redundancy form is emphatically denied.

Befuddled, the porkster lifts his double chin expecting a pink humanised moon in which to fling his poo of gratitude, instead, a grey elderly ape grumbles in his blood-line chair, looking uncomfortably at the infant window gale.

"..Do you know what day it is today?," said Lidman, running a calloused mitt through a thinly existing regimental haircut. "Today.. is my birthday"

Seeking fake emotion, Cod forces a nodding delight.

"Oh..well happy birthday Sir"

"Never let a birthday pass you by Mr. Codbery, especially when you're young. When you become an old, dried up football like me, those mile stones pass like any other day, the gifts get smaller and the candles get bigger...however! mine, have always been special, I'm proud of it too, memories, so many wonderful memories of a better tomorrow, you see my daughter Marian and I share the same birthday and it's kept my fire for it. She's throwing a party for us tonight, at the old family cottage, there is going to be good food, good wine and maybe even a bit of dancing. I'm really looking forward to it Mr. Codbery," Lidman's hairy fist queerly tightens into an angry vibration on the desk. "So I'm sure you can understand that the 'last' 'thing' 'I' 'want' on this day of a-l-l-l days is your overweight, vastly rotund, porking cow of a mother! marching her way up to 'my' front door, manically mooing at me for your immediate reinstatement! Now get back to your desk and work!-work!-work! Before I change my mind Codsbery!!!"

Thunder and fish, a crack of instantaneous fright strikes the Cod flat off the rickety guest chair. bouncing up in a guppy-eyed panic, he flees with relief through the narrow opening, pudge diving the grim staircase back to the deafening, lonely cold comfort of click-clack-click.

Gradually, the silent office returns to its default depression. Rubbing the sore low vertebrae of his furry curve, Lidman yawningly fists a pregnant side cabinet, birthing a rocks liqueur glass, closely chaperoned by its significant other, a proud dazzling half full bottle of Cabin Brown's walnut whiskey. Still rolling his bulbs at the immediate past, he prepares a one inch drink, lifts it gingerly to his mumbling morning mouth and drains it completely. As the last few nutty stinging drops free fall the Bosses oesophagus, he energetically hides the glass back to its sided nook and stands with a newfound sense of speed, out of place from his recent carefully crafted movements of slow intimidation.

Winging the narrow double doors back to beloved solitude, he steals to the howling window, attempting to jiggle-jiggle-jiggle it closed, with each red faced exertion becoming more and more upset and angry, reluctantly letting it lose from his gorilla-ish grip, signalling the jammed pane to come hurtling down with a guillotine slam, missing his sausagey plump thumb by a pixies prick.

"Falling apart! this bloody place...sixty-five, one year, two year and so on, how did that happen? I'm now sixty-five years...old..."

Lid-ing blue lagoons, he presses the frowning frump of his beetle-boss brow against the cold condensation of the window glass, soothing a frontal race-lobe as a raspy female vigour whips his follicle drums from afar.

"You look it as well you ugly git."

Drawing away from the relaxing chill, a soft Lidman revolves to a milling ancient lady, looming out of the smelly dingy dark corridor, bridesmaided by grey cigarette smoke to the tune of a rattling tea tray. Strapped with a haggard handbag, she travels the murky floor with the busy physicality of a war weary Terracotta tank, attacking the old oak desk with cream tea and biscuits, wiping her tobacco stained fingers down a mustard brown pencil skirt that seamlessly camouflages into the peeling wallpaper behind her.

"Having our tea Irish style this morning are we Daniel?" she said, eyeing the walnut whisky trying to blend in amongst the office supplies.

"It's prescription," shrugged DL in a wavering humour. "Stops the back twinges in my crippling old age."

Glaring at him from across the office, her blue-veined back hands pour the boiling Earl Gray into a vapour waving china cup, sitting hotly on a masochistic saucer.

"Give up ya'whingin, you're only a bloody child, do you know where I was on my 65th birthday? Do ya?"

Embracing the airborn result of her smouldering woodbine, Daniel reseats at a newly conjured cafe desk.

"...Let me guess Guiny...you were here?"

"You bet ya'brass balls I was my lad! Holding the fort down stairs, sixty men strong with no breaks, and not once did I say to your Father, 'where's my bollocking birthday cake?' God rest him, and for five long hours I needed the lavy, five bloody hours! The pain, oh the pain, I thought my innards were going to pop, by the time I made it home I was pissing like a storm drain."

"Graphic!..far, far too graphic Guiny."

As Lidman winces his vivid brain box away from the sweet periodic pee push of a woman's toilet, the frail lady hitches up her moth-eaten skirt hem, marching high elbowed to straighten an already perfectly straight portrait, hung three-feet above a boarded up fireplace, its large, garish frame depicting in weathered brush strokes a majestic, grand, gangly seated man with a melted brown moustache, hollow contours and family sapphires of radiant blue with two proud basset hounds standing to attention on either side of a chairman's chair.

"I know ya'gunna think I'm a soppy old slut... but I've bought ya'present, being that it's your birthday and all," said Guin, rotating Boss way with a husky green, tongue cough.

Wormy eyebrowed, D comically slaps his meaty jowl, trying to rouse from a dandelion dream.

"Did I really just hear that, 'Guinevere Troll' has actually bought someone a present, with her o-o-own hard earned money."

Squinting with fury, Guin frantically lights a fresh woodbine from behind her spotted ear.

"Shut ya'gob or I'll smack'ya like I used'ta!; anyway I didn't buy it, It's something that's mine, that I want to give to you, ya'ungrateful little git-git!"

Manoeuvreing forward, she rummages mournfully into the concealed black of her inexpensive handbag. Lidman hiding a genuine intrigue.

"...Lord have mercy, it's not one of your cheese and pickle sandwiches is it?"

"Shut it! Listen for once our'brat...your father, he gave me this when I got married to my old Roger, as a sort of wedding gift..."

With a painful pout, she presents a glinting, six-inch long letter opener, its stubby blade penetrating a leather sheath, its coiled handle morphed into a moody elephants head. Not knowing what to make of the gesture, Daniel delicately accepts the chromed glint in his hairy meat mitts, reading the elegantly engraved letters of 'To My Battle Axe' along one of the tusks.

"It's proper and that, real silver, I've had it checked," said Guiny sharply with a shiver of sadness, as if she had just cut off one of her own fingers. Leaning deskly in a mild discomposure, Lidman shakes a receding bonce.

"Guin I can't take this."

"Course you can ya'gobby bastard, just put it in ya'pocket."

"Why would you give this to me Guiny?...it was engraved for you..."

Wrinkled lips tucking to a thin line of tightness, she twists her flat comfortable loafs into the office floor, pondering how best to express herself.

"..Well since Roger...ya'know, last year, kicked the bucket and all that, I've been thinking a lot about things and my position and what not, to say that I'm old now would be a bit of an understatement, a bloody relic's more like it, and when I eventually shuffle off as it were, I'm afraid to say the group of ground vultures that I suppose would be considered my nearest and dearest, will ransack my little hovel faster than you can say 'she's dead doctor'. And to be honest it doesn't really bother me...it never has, you can't take it with you, so if they want the lot, they can have every bloody stick of it...but not this, I'm not letting them have this, there's three little trinkets that are very dear to me, and this is one of them, so instead of it landing in the lap of my brother Stan, who would be biting at the bit, to melt it down in time for market the next morning, I'd like to give it to you...you're the only one I'd ever give it to..."

Reluctant, respectful and touched by rare sentiment, Lidman rehomes the precious elephanto in the tweeded care of his breast pocket as Guiny rapidly blinks, ancient wedding day tears back to their toughened ducts, opting instead for a gummy, yellowish smile that hurriedly melts upon acknowledging the untouched barley biscuits.

"Oi! get on with eating them!, a whole shilling they cost.."

"...I'm resisting, need to save my gut for tonight." said D sipping his tea, avoiding the small floating flakes of kettle born limescale while showing a routine enjoyment to an arms akimbo Guin.

"A party is it? who's coming to muddy ya'floor then?"

"Well I'll be there obviously, my chum Larry from the NCA and maybe a few other members, I think Marian's got a couple of work friends coming, who have I missed out..oh yes, my neighbour Mrs. Betridge and her son have been invited as well, and that's about it I'm afraid."

Guin puff-puffs with the expression of a smelled fart.

"Well don't expect me to pad out the guest list, it's me Friday night! I'll be down Lamb and Duck with Beryl Miggs, they're doing Irish folk night with meat pies!"

With great eccentricity, the frail lady jumps into an odd combination of Kabuki theatre and Morris dancing, running short of breath in a matter of seconds to indulge in a phlegm filled coughing fit as she corrals the bone china, drinking the dregs of Earl Gray left in Lidman's cup followed by a crammed biscuit.

"What's the NCA anyway?!" she asked, spraying a dazzling display of avian crumbs.

"Stands for The National Coin Association, I'm head of committee for their Birmingham branch," swelled DL with a pinch of pride.

"You'wa? So ya'just meet up like and look at grubby grey coins together...in a big huddle?"

"Well...In a way yes, but they're very old coins Guin, Spanish reales, Portuguese tangas, Saxon penny's, each one a little wee piece of the past... they're fascinating."

"Well it sounds like a right chuffing crack I hope never to witness, hey with any luck I'll be counting my own penny's tonight...at the bar that is!!!"

Erupting in a crazy eyed cackle, she slides the dying woodbine to the crusted corner of her spluttering, biscuity grin, elevates the weighty tea tray with winged elbows and courageously tanks her noisy, one woman band, back down the shadow bound corridor, her smoke lingering laugh eventually fading away with a selfless symphony of clinking porcelain.

Alone again, thinking of tonight and attempting to avoid for a brief jiffy, the morning pile of awaiting paperwork, Daniel confronts the grizzled wall clock with a breathy procrastination before a freshly injected pen hand hits the first quotation. Steadily he works-works-works all through the day, banning his old blues from the Medusered quarterly face, beaming from its high hooked position, and despite its timely siren song tempting him once or twice, the towering paper cut pile, diminishes lower and lower until the scribbling fountain is startled still by an aggressively shrill home bell reaching its daily orgasm from the lower floor.

Creaking free from a muscly desk lean, Lidman's painfully rigid neck adjusts to a forward cannonball of disorientation.

"Five! Can't be five already?...Can it?"

Strong and pungent, the pickley cheese scent of an untouched sandwich, coldly placed on the edge of the desk, the last unwanted remnants of a 2:30 break, completely forgotten. Rubbing the aching numb of his tree trunk thighs, the rummy long hand flicks past the five, prompting a semi-confident knock at the solitudious doors. Quickly the potent sandwich joins the hiding wet whisky glass as Mr. Lidman frantically grabs the closest form to hand and starts ticking an already ticked list of staff lavatory maintenance.

"Come in!" he exclaimed, returning to a mean, militant boom as Mr. Richmore's fake, thin, skeleton grin hangs into view.

"Very productive day Sir, we done well, forty-two quotes and booted a good ten percent off the backlog." asserted Richmore, flaring his nostrils, trying to detect where the pong of pickle is coming from.

"Adequate! but not good enough," growled the grim Chairman from a familiar heavy hunch.

"We're behind, I want to be ahead by Friday next...any reservations Mr. Richmore?"

"Absolutely not Sir, they'll get it done, or god help them I'll..."

"Good! That will be all," interrupted D, dropping his severe sop to repeatedly ring the random sentence, 'End stall in dire need of new ballcock'.

Listening to his number two hurriedly flush down the grandeur stairs, Lidman waits for the full evacuation of clerks to muse in his hairy shells before happily disposing of his sequestered, smelly bin sandwich. Clothing his bouldered shoulders with a long grey leaving coat and tough gloves of black pig leather, stealing onto the spacious landing, he grants a solicitous site to the neverending rain attacking the office window, damning his lack of foresight as well as an absent umbrella.

By and by, the highs and goodbyes of the grand staircase complete the old man's prospering way across the shadowy mottled brown aisle, the floor once colonized by paper roll mountains now completely empty, its vast lonesomeness only comforted by the filtered sun, shining its pampered rods through the lengthy left windows to lay rest over the dark hall of abandoned adding machines, each sheathed with individual strength dust covers.

Massaging a tight pinch in his shirted barrel chest, the ghostly inner alcove, cuddles his tempered grunt to the oversized baton brass handles. Predicting a powerful vacuum from the whirling wild wind, Lidman swells his well of quiet rage, clamping the twin brass with two simian dukes and with an elderly roar wrenches them open to greet the home-time world of honking car horns and the delicate spit of dusk lit rain droplets. U-turning back to the door, long coat dancing to the tempo of any and all airstreams of warm storm humidity, he locks his family innards with a long key length of distressed copper, freeing up a ruing fist.

"Bloody foreign weather!"

Waterlogged and pea green in colour, a venerable old Ford, parked to near sand stone, tiredly awaits as DL clogs down the stone steps to meet it soggy glisten. Doubling up his wide body with a dirty, embryonic slam, the orchestral sounds of homebound vehicles become muffled, mild and minky. Ignition turned, the ride of rotten interior gives a half-hearted rev before dying into obscurity. forced to try again the car gives a faint metallic clang from deep inside its failing combustion. utterly irked, Daniel tiredly squeezes the sweaty thin ridges of Mr. steering wheel.

"You o-o-nly have one job, one thing to do in life and I expect it done well...start! or you're scrap!"

Assuredly the cowering old transport complies, shuddering to life with a loud unhealthy petrol moan, careering onto the bleak high street and driving a shade of pea green into the rapidly brief landscape, the multi-greyed market stalls being packed away, the red rolling apples in the gushing gutter, the locked and local library, all painted a golden glaze by the hot dying sun, beaming bright in the low sky, fighting the hungry horizon for a long lasting dwindle. Travelling for twenty-three minutes out of the coal black metropolis, passing rustic pubs and muddy mingles, the surrounding landmarks becoming less evolved, less populated and vastly untamed, the filthy wheels spinning with high velocity down a thin country lane, bullied by dense bramble bushes running raw against the rusted car handles.

Eager to embrace home and Daughter, the birthday boy ankles the speed, tackling a virgin bend at a walloping thirty, sharp thorn needles slashing along the flaking green paintwork as a blur of red fur dashes from the thick pube-ish bramble across the narrow wet road in close proximity to the hurtling pea green ford, its glowing vaporous headlamps illuminating the fright filled face of a young fox cub, losing faith in its good pace, frozen with fear, its parting little jaw growing wider and wider as old man D, gaspingly stomps a screeching pedal to bring the car to an immediate halt, but it's too-too late, the fox is too young and the brakes are too old, the poor cubs body temporarily lifts the back axle as the dragging, guilt filled Ford finally scourers its gritish tires to a shivering stand still.

Sitting stunned with up and down lungs, Lidman wipes his heavily frowned forehead with a shaking leather palm, turning his big bottom to face the matted pile of red burgundy still twitching in the distance.

Foreseeing in a solemn stare that the oozing animal will be dead within the hour, he starts the ragged motor with a held breath and continues in a driving haste to his fated celebration. But here and now, free and alive, behind the wheel of a rushing green pea, blissfully unaware of just how lucky fox cubs can be.

CHAPTER TWO:

The Cottage

Seraphim buds, sing and salivate around the safe baked aroma of warm and delicious iced buns, served in a country cottage kitchen, brilliantly basted walnuts covered in melted milk chocolate taking their rightful place alongside puffy and sumptuous scones smeared with thick cream and freshly made strawberry jam, all diligently displayed on a lengthy, party table of perfect plates by sultry and slender hands of china white, belonging to a young woman of twenty-three all busy limbs in the pursuit of perfection, laying down plate after plate of taste bud tempting torments so gently onto the lilac lace tablecloth beneath.

Her clothes, an odd assortment of shouldered cooking cloth and ragged remnants of a finished work day, the straight mention of a skirt, sensible shoes and the prominent peek of a creased, untucked blooming blouse shirt unabashedly visible on the peripheral sides of a populated pinny of various stains.

Rerolling a fallen sleeve back up to her elegant elbow, a three-inch faded stretch of letters, scribbled at a forty-five degree angle along the side of her wrist in careful ink pen, 'Welcome to the Queens Hotel, my name is Marian, how can I help you today,' followed by the illegible dictation 'shoulders back remember to smile'.

Spotting a fellow smell, the sweet tabled aroma surrounding her homely habit, climbs in a ballet of scent to mingle with the looming waft of sinister oven smoke. A flapping fume of burning sugar flies up her dainty nostrils, fueling a wide eyed remembrance of a frail fruit pie forgotten in flames and embracing its neglect as a consequence.

The side of the table, impacted by a dropped plate of boring biscuits, welcomes the ceramic clunk as she rushes over, tea towel in tow to rescue the puff pastry from complete incineration.

"Please don't be burnt! Please don't be burnt!" said Marian, hastily.

As the oven door is yanked open by its blistering, towel covered hot knob, sooted exhaust leaps with igneous air into the wincing shade of her blue ocean-berry eyes, provoking a stylish cough, cough, sniffle cough while brushing a wavy ringlet of caramel blonde away from her heavenly heart shaped face.

Looking longingly to the ended egg timer, she retrieves the medium sized baking tray to admire with a wrapped grip, the sad shedding shape of charcoal, smoldering with smoke wings at its center.

"Nobody likes pear pie anyway" she said in a shrugging huff, scraping and shaking the hot onyx lump into the home bin.

Upon bowing her build of tall and slender, over the sink to ventilate the quaint and spacious kitchen with the aid of an opened window, she turns lightheaded with the heat, quickly saved by a cool breeze accompanied by dwindling sunlight and thin veils of rain lightly kissing the window sill.

Before Leaving the tap and basin in pursuit of the living room, Marian tosses her newly unknotted cooking apron into a wall bearing wicker basket, placed within falling distance of the mud stained mat protecting the front door.

Crossing the full span of the kitchen in a breathy, beautiful glide, she passes the plentiful dessert table until doorway under head, her footing switches from tastefully tiled to the rich ruby carpet of the living room. A large cosy affair of comfortable furniture complete with old grand piano and messy fireplace, a chaise lounge of deepest navy stretching its way to a quarterly stocked drinks cabinet and a brightly lit, coffee coloured corridor leading off to a separate poignant part of the commodious cottage.

The lounging layout is transformed for the evening by a single festive line of colourful bunting, skirting all four walls and a big bay window before finishing listlessly limp at the foot of a solitary staircase running parallel to the wall.

Floating a mired sigh, Marian deeply reclines her tired backside into a leather green arm chair. Curtained by chin length waves, she lightly massages the nape of her swan-like neck with a fair right hand of romance, while reaching with a prominent left towards a peculiar item perched proudly atop an elevated side table.

Seventeen centimetres in height, resembling a miniature wine barrel suspended on its side within a sturdy stand, she places a fluid finger on its top and spins the mysterious rolodex in the manner that a cat would bat a ball of yarn. Revolving on a horizontal axis it begins to click faster and faster, click-click-click, as its internal vocation slowly comes to an end, the barrel stops dead, signalling from its middle the drop of a doll house door, displaying a freshly rolled cigarette.

Lit with a nearby matchbox, Marian coquettishly clamps two bow lips of a plump design around its lower waist, breathing in a shimmering drag, a brief hold before exhaling she kicks off her shoes, rolling each laddered stock from a lengthy pin, enabling the rough rub between her bare aching feet and the knobbly leg of a blushing foot stool.

Slumping further still, she lays back with patient purity, her family jewels covered with lowered lashes, listening intently to the big bay window, drone on and on about drips, drops and Macbethian blackbirds.

A weary knock-knock tremors the heavy front door, making the mud stained mat stand to attention. Marian's languorous oval eyes snap open with growing pupils. sitting up in an instant, she cig-stubs a kinky ashtray of circular cut glass and gazelles back into the kitchen.

Reaching the mat in a happy hop, she slides the front doors rectangular, peep panel to one side, down gazing the sodden site of a damp and disgruntled Daniel J. Lidman.

"What's the password!" yelled Marian, imitating a doorman severity.

Fatherly irises raise to the rectangle in a weary yet jovial slant proceeded by a mumbling baritone.

"A big glass of wine...red."

"...It was actually 'pogostick' but close enough."

Shutting away her fruity framed grin, M opens the entrance with doting paws, a lead footed DL wading in with a succession of groans to hang his coat on a cluttered hat rack, receiving a warm, drying, daughterly hug upon the turn of his haggard heels.

"Happy birthday lass... we really need another door key."

"Well stop losing yours then. Happy birthday dad..."

"...It's colder than a witches tit out there...it's in weather such as this, I'm glad that I'm human..."

Shivering his load bearing build over the turning tune of a swift relocking, DL's thinning twin brows ups and ups again when confounded by the glorious display of sugar along the lengthy kitchen table.

"Bloody hell girl! Sweets'a'plenty, we'll have to hide most of this until after the main, or they'll be full up on buns before it's ready," he said, eyeing up seven jam tarts on a provocative platter.

"I told you last night were having a Fête douce," retorted M in a flowing French accent, a fuddled Father peering back at the winking tarts.

"A fat what?"

"It's a dessert party Dad! Marie Antoinette invented it in the seventeenth century, it was all the rage in Paris, I asked you last night and you said crackin. Why don't you ever listen to me?"

"Ho-ho-hold on a second…you mean this is it? The only thing we have to offer them, cake, alcohol and more cake, they'll have no teeth by the end."

"I know isn't it wonderful!," smiled Marian with patty cake palms. "Right, I've ironed one of those brown shirts I bought for you last week, it's nicely folded on your bed and be quick as a fox, we haven't got long before people start turning up."

"I hate them shirts. Collars are sharp, they rub my neck red raw, I'm fine in what I'm wearing, it's you who needs to get changed and how did reception go?..."

"Well you should have told me they were sharp... I have to smile for six-hours but it pays better than being a maid did, anyway don't change the subject, you can't wear that it's..."

Her linguistic flow is struck down by the sight and sound of an orangey, freckled hand rapping at the kitchen window with a tap-tap-tap. Retreating away from the sink, she catches the bobbing glimpse of a balding head, wrapped by a wiry, laurel wreath of thin ginger hair, intertwined with semi-translucent lines of grey and silver.

"Oh god it's that man you collect coins with, the creepy one, he's always creepin'..."

Backing away further, nervously patting her hourglass thighs, she discovers a break-time smoke stick, still laying idle in the velvet lining of her work skirt pocket.

Ape stepping to the heavy oak entrance, Daniel slides the shutter to address the spotted splendour haunting the stoop, complete with reddish roman nose, thick rim glasses and a clotted cardigan of buff brown wool, complementing a boring brain of foam and thin air apart from coins and collectables, all delightfully topped off by a low lipped crusted cold sore.

"What's the password Larry?"

Befuddled by Lidman's greeting, the red-headed Chum admits a dim line of lullaby blinks to match his fallen guppy gob.

"Password? Oh right...I didn't think we needed one, shall I go then?" Replied the Chum in a high male voice, the tedious tone limp and whiny to a frowning rectangle.

"Don't be a wet teabag ya'towny fool, it's just a bit of fun!"

"Fun...I thought as much, but passwords can be important," Larry added to an opening hinge invite.

Advancing the warm scullery with a queer fussy wiggle, the ferret-like guest corrects his poor posture upon the fair mirage of a casual Marian, bare foot in her grubby work clothes, attempting to relight a bent Camel cigarette on the yellow ring stove.

"You remember Marian don't you Larry? She was singing your praise not one second ago," smirked Daniel, enduring the hot-hive of a daughter's squinting sting.

"Greetings Marian," wooed the Ferret, rocking back on his heels. "May I say you look particularly pretty this evening, a right Aphrodite, that's the Greek goddess of love you know."

Departing from a cringe worthy compliment, she inhales a lung full of impatience to exhale her exit.

"Is it really, well I can't stand around gabbing, need to get ready, I'm sure Father will fix'ya a sipper..."

Hurriedly leaving the kitchen to tread red ruby, she swoops the banister and zips upstairs to the pink, safe sanctuary of her bedroom.

In a flash, Mr. Lidman turns ripe, child-like and highly animated towards Larry's odd occupation of collectable interest.

"Have you got it then? Have you brought it with you?"

"...Plucked it from the glass case yesterday," fretted Larry. "I'm not accustomed to taking museum property for a stroll, If I didn't own the exhibit I could be severely reprimanded."

"Yes-yes but have you got it?, on your person, now."

Inspired by the Hostly hype, the ginger grump lifts a weak gimp chin to a proud nobility.

"...Affirmative, and I will allow you to hold it, however no living soul must know, it's arguably the most valuable item we have on display and I don't appreciate being called a wet tea bag..."

Slipping a probing index inside his buff brown cardigan to reach the near pocket of an off-white shirt, Larry's returning arm produces a tiny, square, manila envelope packet, haltingly handing it to a lit up Lidman who lays its weighty circumference flat in his primitive palm.

"It's heavier than I expected, such a little thing too. Can I open it then? I'll be very gentle..."

Receiving a reluctant nod of consent, the envelope is tenderly peeled and its contents exposed; exhausted and subtly silver, a timely ravaged coin of blackish green.

"Well as I live and shit. The rarest Greek coin ever found eh', stunning, absolutely stunning, the life it must have had...how old did you say it was?"

Enchanted, DL examines the minute detail of two Hellenes soldiers clutching a dead rabbit beneath a great Grecian sun.

"Well it was dug up on the island of Samos," puffed the Grump, reciting his tour guide patter. "So, we estimate the Hellenic Navy would have pressed them around 7th century BC. But these days it's retired on a comfy wooden plaque, well... until you made me pluck-pluck"

Embracing a high zenith, Lidman's craving want appears in heavy breathing. His greedy gorilla grip, encloses the currency in a hairy, hugging sque-e-e-ze. "A coin like this in my collection would make me very happy...how much do you want for it?"

Larry's mouth, eyes and even his nose holes, widen at the mere mention of a perverted price.

"...I can't sell it to you, absolutely not, that's property of the Birmingham Collection Centre, it's been lent from the big willy's in London, if that coin went missing, they'd turn their back on Brum forever."

"Nonsense! No one will notice, just look at it, it's practically a speck, and it is my birthday after all."

Lidman gives a further squeeze to Larry's dismay.

"I would notice! It goes against my principles and such, now if it's all the same to you, I think I better have it back…"

Swallowed up by a great grey whale of uncomfortable silence, the cowering coin is timidly returned to Larry's peeved possession, repackaged and sequestered once more beneath a thick layer of buff brown wool. Attempting to leave via a blow hole of awkwardness, Daniel playfully slaps the red Ferret's shoulder, adding a manufactured laugh.

"Drinks I think! Most definitely, what do you fancy? We have both kinds of wine or a fine Scottish whisky, you can have a Brandy or maybe a..."

"Brandy's for after meals," said L, cutting him off, still arranging his nipple coin through ripples of buff.

"True-is Larry, a warmed up Brandy should only be consumed after a good hearty meal, unfortunately there is no good meal coming our way, hearty or otherwise, the only food we have to eat this evening is on that table over there..."

Daniel delegates towards the lengthy, pudding pile responsible for Larry's quizzical face shape.

"But that's children's food!"

"Ye-e-es I know it's unconventional, but Marian thought it would be apple dandy if everyone could ski down their dentist bill for the next ten years...it's all the rage in France apparently."

Upon hearing the nourishing name of his caramel crush, Larry's cheeks begin to sport a pinkish blend, struggling to be prominent amongst the rashy wrinkles.

"Marian's idea was it? Well if the French do it…I might nibble a biscuit."

"…Oh sod it! I'm actually going to do it, I'm having a brandy, a hot brandy, I really mean it Larry, don't try and stop me!" cried a labouring Lidman, desperate to inject a level of zazz into the dull day banter, lumbering his rock log body into the living room to hassle the bunting bound bottles with a witty whistle.

Left cleaning his spectacles, the copper headed Ferret conjures the fleeting thought of eating an iced bun, swiftly dismissing such idle debauchery. His bubble of self abuse popped in turn by a bounding birthday boy returning with two highballs and a wide wasted bottle of Constantino brandy, peeling his most mocking impression of a cave dwelling Neanderthal.

"Now we make fire! ugg!-ugg!-ugg!"

Queuing Constantino and co along the precarious kitchen counter, Daniel brings out a small candle warmer. His back turned in lighting, pouring, preparation, he flairs a quiet question into the air.

"Just out of interest...that Samos coin, if it ended up in an auction, which I know it wouldn't, but hypothetically speaking, how much would it sell for do you think...?"

Under mental protest, Larry ponders the math, watching the first tenderly turned highball, a seductive flame licking its curved convexity.

"...Well as long as its hypothetical...it's quite hard to say really, some of the sale would go to the coordinating company, you would be taxed of course and I think the National Treasury seeks a piece as well, that being said if the coin was illegally sold on the black market, I imagine it would fetch something along the lines of... fifty.. fifty-five thousand pounds."

Lidman propellers round with bulging blues.

"Fifty!!! For that little coin!"

"...Oh most definitely, that's the Treasury's quote for it, it's mostly down to its remarkable condition, it's the rabbit's teeth, the suns outline, a foreign collector would snatch it up."

"That's madness, insane, crazy, Fifty-thousand pounds!...I'm all for investing in'yow collection but that truly is bonkers money!"

Pausing, D allows the lay of his bubbling blood pressure, reviving the calm decorum of a good host, handing a warm brandy glass to Chum.

"For instance...in my collection upstairs I happen to have an 1878 Spanish Centimo that I paid a market merchant thirty pounds for."

Impressed, Ferret nods in a cultured smug.

"1878...does it show the two kings of Spanish Succession trying to strangle each other?"

"It does inde-e-ed Larry, fancy hav..."

All of a sudden, in an instant and without any warning whatsoever, a loud, hellish, metallic toned honking, sounds off outside the rain ridden cottage, drawing ever closer to the fainting front door, booming with the old world blow of a hunting horn, distilling such a sudden inhale of panic that Larry drops his shuddering brandy glass, tumbling down-down-down, the highball smashes into a million tiny pieces over the kitchen floor, firing translucent shards and splattered brandy in every direction as birthday boy Lidman clutches a tight chest in a melting moment of profound, panting, wide eyed bewilderment, the incessant honk!-honk!-honk! crescendos with a crash followed by a faint cracking sound, leaving the house reverberating in a frightening, dying, fantasia of screaming rim rubber and roaring relocated ravens.

"What in hell!!!" yelled the gasping Gorilla from a new, low tiled position.

As the sound dust settles to a nil numb note, a second turbulent tide begins as Marian run stomps across the landing and scrabbles down the staircase with an elated teenage squeal. Hurtling round the banister, she bursts in the view to Father and Ferret, gliding towards the scene wearing an emerald green tassel dress, star lit by sequins and yelling at the top of her lovely lungs.

"She's here! She's here!"

With a kitten-limb kick, M leaps the sharp, glassy floor to pounce and fling the lock and front door wide open, disappearing into the cold, dusky, aqueous air to greet the sensational source.

Still recovering, D and L exchange a toey look followed by a leaned look, through the chilly opened entrance, the framed apparition of thick, billowing black engine smoke, quickly eclipsed by Marian's returning outline heavenly haloed by a setting sun.

Rose petal lips lifted in a feline glee, she carries the crude wrap of a botched birthday present, her rear closely pursued by the small shouldered shadow of a little girl, tottering five-foot tall and wrapped in a beige trench coat, her dolly bonce, a magazine trend assortment of jet black crow feathers, emanating the corner of a ruby red headscarf.

Scurrying alongside Marian with a mousy apprehension, the sidling child comes closer into social proximity, showing by shades, fades and a slight fall of collagen, that she is in fact in the very early Eden of her twenties.

Standing slack jawed, the Lidman Larry duo fail to greet or even acknowledge the new button nosed babe over the meandering smoke cloud, orbiting the heavy front door, its coughing gape hastily shut-locked again by birthday girl M.

"...Father this is Ethel, we work at the Hotel together."

Bemused, Daniel looks down at the little guest.

"...Yes, I remember you sayin'such," he murmured. "Nice to meet you young lady, Marian tells me your family owns the Queens, that must be worth a few bob..."

Turning irate, the doorway Daughter feebly fumes at a money minded Father for revealing her gossiping breach.

Fighting her shyness, Ethel responds in a bundle of eek's.

"Hello I'm Ethel! Happy Birthday, I only got Marian a present, I didn't know what you wanted, sorry about your tree by the way."

"What tree!?" barked Lidman, startling the ranting Mouse.

"Nothing! never mind! Wow look at all those cakes, they look delicious, why is there glass all over the floor? I got her a scarf, she said she wanted a scarf!"

Wary of litigious layman's, Daniel surveys the granulated radius of dried brandy as Marian forward treads a crisping crack, under her two-inch heels.

"Yes why is there glass over the floor?...I'll sweep it up."

Concerned, Father webs out his arms.

"Don't be stupid girl, I'm doing it, now everyone into the Living Room unless you want a nasty shard of glass, stuck in your foot. Show them the new music player or something of the like.."

An agreeing Daughter ushers Ethel towards the cosy threshold, plating an iced bun each before seeking out a comfortable nest in which to consume them, followed in red rat toe by a biscuit grabbing Larry.

Now solo with the reflecting comfort of one's own self, Daniel walks the Constantino tiles to open a walk in pantry, which conveniently borrows from the adjacent Living Room, the sloping space under the staircase for tins, cans, various cleaning products, forgotten fishing rods and a thick bristled broom, dragged from its working class slumber to break its back for the big bad boss.

Sweeping the shards into one corner of the kitchen in a friendly flashback of boy time chores, he spots a large piece of shattered highball, sparkling with glassy prick lights under the dessert table. Groaning, he bambi's down, crawling under the lilac lace to pincer the princely prick just as Marian reenters.

"Are you sure you don't need any help?... were ya'gone?, oh you're down there."

"Little bastard was trying to escape! Where's the pan?" muffled D, reversing his bread roll build from under a frilly cascade of lilac, soon helped to a swaying head rush by kitty cat M.

"Just leave it Dad, I'll pan it later-late, now will you please come into the Living Room, your creepy friend is telling a story about getting lost in East Grinstead, it's unbearable!"

Escapee joining its fellow menacing jags, Marian forcefully pulls a dizzy headed Father into the Ferret's dull domination.

Miserably slumped in the smallest armchair offered up by the bunting bliss, Ethel nibbles with a doll-like hand the rough crust of her disappearing iced bun, suffering the torturous tedium of Larry's neverending adventure.

"So then I had to go down Newbery road because Felbridge avenue had flooded the day before, but then I realised that the farmers market was also open on a Tuesday, so as you would expect I was held up behind a tractor for a good ten minutes or was it fourteen minutes..."

Reaching her limit, a mousy Ethel leaps from her seat, to the brand new Gramophone under the big bay window.

"Can we play music on the machine Marian?"

"Oh Yes, for the love of God yes!" said M, leaping likewise.

Leisurely, Daniel proclaims his usual throne, a large, imposing, downy brown grandfather chair, directly opposite a protesting Ferret, perversely stroking an uneaten biscuit.

"But if you mess around with that spinner thing, you won't be able to hear the rest of my sto..."

New age music immediately and gratefully interrupts the red ratigan's tail, the powerful, scatty, beat Jazz sound of smooth sax, trumpet and trombone follow piano and drum, linking arm in arm with gay abandon, leaping out of the brass horn flower into all manner of unregulated notes as Cat and Mouse converse in high, girlish giggles, purring, squeaking and pouring wild berry wine by the quarterly stocked drinks cabinet, there milk and honey huffs peeping through every domineering Jazz note, about how dreamy and perpetually topless Douglas Fairbanks was in his last movie, suggestively titled 'The Thief of Baghdad'.

Wincing with projection, DL attempts to chum chat over the beat bop tones.

"So, what do you think of the Cottage Larry?!"

"Weeds!"

"...Pardon!"

"Weeds! You have a lot of weeds outside!"

"Yes I know about the weeds! I was referring to the inside!"

"Oh…yes it's quite pleasant! A real grand country cottage, it reminds me of a Berkshire guest house I stayed in while attending my auntie Ann's funeral, it was a delightful stay, the sheets were spotless, the management was polite and well mannered, you're bleeding by the way, the food was a bit potato heavy but the carrots were cooked to perfection"

As Larry continues on about pineapple scented soap in the bathroom being a step to far, Daniel inspects the end of the chair arm, noticing and then pronto feeling a small but cleanly sliced lesion, throbbing the tip of his middle finger, admitting a steady drip-drip-drip of red rouge onto the light, beige coloured rug beneath.

Quickly gob sucking his stubby digit, trying to avoid a Daughter's dismay, he maneuvers an oaky chair leg over the growing, golf ball sized stain, now taking to rest in a pale maze of fine fibers.

Slow to respond, Larry acknowledges his lack of concern.

"You should do something about that, don't you think?"

"Your stupid glass, your clumsiness, my bloody finger" whispered DL, sharply.

"Yes, I think that's what's happened as well... apologies."

Carried by domestic Jazz to the centre of the room, Marian pretends to dance with an invisible prince charming, waltzing around the chairs with a swilling white wine bottle.

"Would anyone like a refreshment?"

"Nothing for me, I not drink no more, problem with belly," said Larry, infuriating a near seated Host.

"You don't drink!, well you might have told me, that brandy's expensive and although it may be a very conventional usage, I intended for it to be drunk! Not to add a glossy glint to my kitchen floor!"

Whether it was Daniel's belligerent tone, Larry's new found guilt, a discomforted Marian or Ethel's rotten remembrance of being given brandy as a child to make her sleep, the bunting room slips into an abnormal yet familiar silence, lasting far beyond the reaches of natural rumination before being unexpectedly broken by a slithering creak coming from upstairs.

Unsettled, the Mouse's leaning curiosity hones in on the looming shadow at the top of the solitary staircase.

"Is there someone else here?"

"No-no it's just us, this is a very old house, likes to make noises, I've always put it down to the fact, that most of the main beams are from dismantled sailing ships," remarked Lidman, casually.

Discomposed by the ship house trivia, Ethel shoots a concerned look at the ceiling for fear of it caving in as a white wine Marian soothes and disparages the statement.

"Don't believe him Ethel, he's joking"

"I'm not joking at all Lass. seventy odd years ago, down Southampton docks, they finished taking apart all the big wooden boats to make way for the future. Chinese boats, American boats, Spanish, French, all ended up in a great pile of timber. People came from all over to build houses out of it, look you can even see where one of the iron assembly pegs went in."

Lidman points out a gaping square hole in the black beam above the threshold. Its queer, non nature shape widening Ethel's anxious eyes to their maximum peepage.

"Maybe the haunted souls of deceased sailors are trapped inside the wood, and by building them into your home, they walk around at night, opening doors, trying to find their long lost Captain…"

"Oh thanks Ethel! Why did you have to say that, I'm not going to be able to sleep tonight," moaned the Cat, taking a big gulp of her cottage white.

Embracing the philosophical fun, Father's accountancy brain booms its loud logic.

"Rubbish!, the idea of ghosts walking about, isn't it Larry?"

"I remember now, it was a Friday" said red Rat in a dim day dream.

"What? We're talking about ghosts Larry."

"Ghosts?...Yes nasty little buggers."

"I was just saying it's all a load of nonsense."

"They're not nonsense!," Said the Mouse carrying on. "I even have proof of their existence, only to myself though. It was something unexplainable and impossible that happened when I was four, it was the middle of the night, moonlight coming through the curtains and I vividly recall it was deadly silent and then I heard something moving on the floor, I sat up in bed and all my toys started to come alive."

"Ethel, I love you...you're a wonderful person...but I hate you, my room's full of toys," sighed Marian, practically inhaling her last sweet berry dregs and lunging cabinet way for a refill.

As Ethel reflects further on a tattered memory, her biddy pumps together with little pink pins, fall short of the carpet, dangling around the weathered chair legs.

"It's the most terrified I've ever been before or since, a sort of paralysed, milky white type feeling. Parents thought I dreamt it of course, but I remember one detail so clearly it couldn't have been a dream...in my room there was a porcelain mold of a teddy bear holding a bunch of balloons, it was a children's wall decoration hung on a hook...and I remember it going up and down, up and down, up and down."

A mark of ungodliness, those last repeated words, strangely unnerving to old man D. Enduring the chilly twitch of every thick grey follicle, his bullying blues lift to the windy bay as the rain picks up, the sun exists but only just as two caring crows land on the sill outside the window, black as night with winged warnings, grabbing the attention of everyone inside, squawk!-squawk!-squawk! go the crows, tapping their peck protrusions on the glass, the last of many ill-omens sent throughout the day, screaming with bill tears for what is to come and once again, completely and irreversibly ignored.

CHAPTER THREE:

Young Males

T he wild wind despairs in front of the
ready rain for finishing its storm duties
for the evening, leaving in its wake freshly
laid oblate dew on every log and leaf, the sun
dwindling down to its last remaining beams, the
pale orange glow, glinting off the sea blue bonnet of a carefully driven motor, its combustion
of engine bearings and piston rings playing its
automation song of dominant dives and flaring
phoenix fires, up and down, up and down, up
and down, turning with precise accuracy around
the tight corners of a country lane. Passing by an
abandoned Car nestled at the foot of a grassy

scenic path entitled Navis Lane by a white wash sign post, two garish driving gloves, confidently command the wheel with virile gusto, both tailored to fit the ten and two grip of a fashionable young male of twenty-eight, his athletic frame of fine muscle rippling neck way to short back and sides, surrounding fair hair of chestnut, its floppy thickness sufficiently combed to an indented side parting. In the passenger seat beside him, there sits a thin, prim, buzzard woman of similar age and expensive style, her strikingly dark features, proper and poised beneath a ruler straight fringe of darkest ebony. Scratching her bold beak, she stares at the thick, borderline bushes passing as a muddy brambled blur, the faint ring of her name being called repeatedly cutting into her mental musings of high hygiene and the lack thereof in her current surroundings.

"Margo...I say Margo!"

"...Yes dear?"

"I said whose party are we going to?"

Undernourished by hidden bulimia, the bird of perfect posture shakes her head derisively, replying in a semi-polished diction, a strangled grain of Brummie under every passing vowel.

"Ben I'm not telling you again, it's Marian's, you met her last summer."

"Oh your blonde friend is it? Nice girl, was she the one you brought along to Bournville to see me and Smithy play in the Warwickshire cricket final and I hit a six and the two of you couldn't handle the heat and left without telling us..."

Forward facing, Margo drops the vocality of her response, opting instead for a slow agreeable nod in Ben's side eye.

"Well let's hope she likes the painting set, still boggles my bonnet about the cufflinks though."

"They're not for her Ben, it's her father's birthday as well."

"On the same day!? That sounds like a bit of bad luck if you ask me, I wouldn't much fancy it, when my day comes around it's all about Benjo!" said the Stallion with a slight sided smile, pointing a muscular thumb at himself.

"She said she likes it, it's nice that they share a day together."

"Suppose it's easier on the old chaps wife, two party's with only half the mess."

Upon the buck, Margo's demeanour quickens with relief.

"Ah you've just reminded me of something… Marion's mother isn't around anymore, passed away from typhus during the War, so if she comes up in conversation just be respectful, in fact don't say anything at all, just to be on the safe side, quite an amazing woman actually, she was one of the V.A.D nurses sent over to front line France."

Agreeable mumbles chew from Ben's horsey chomp, his full attention reading a poorly painted road sign, flying by at thirty.

"Right darling, get the mappy ready, we're getting close, we're looking for a sign saying Nollow something, something."

Margo runs her wedding ringed hand talon along a pre-prepared script of scraggly roads.

"Navis? It's Navis Lane, we have already passed it…"

"No we haven't Dear, I remember coming this way a year ago, I'm sure I saw a cottage up ahead."

"It's back there I'm telling you," said Margo, prodding the map. "Ben stop the car and turn around, look we are here on Gullivers street, we turned left a few minutes ago, there was a car parked...it must have been that filthy little lane."

"...Are you sure? It's an awful lot of effort to turn around if you're wrong."

"Yes I'm sure!! Now turn around, we are late as it is!"

"All right, all right, no need to shout darling, there's a good girl."

Buckishly, Ben pulls the brand new brakes, taming the tires to a halt. Performing the necessary manoeuvres, they speed off back the way they came, twenty yards, fifty yards, hundred yards. Drawing near to the correct, overgrown turning, their faithful landmark, the grassy banked Car has disappeared, its non-ness clocked and then stamped as irrelevant by a mild Margo as she applies a light cloud of powdered makeup to her sharp bone structure.

The motor's suspension is put to the test as it rattles down the muddy pebble and rock infested lane. Cornering a wet bend, the magnificent Cottage emerges like a peek-a-boo child from behind the wide trunk of a wind weary oak tree.

Sitting on a rock, greeting them at the foot of a grey gravel drive, a four-foot tall, algae covered stone statue of Pan playing pipes, feeling in its motionless matter an eternal shame at its earthly restrictions, contemplating all the pain it could have prevented on this dreadful day of days.

Unseasonable yellow and dead red leaves, litter the ground as the narrow spokes turn into the drive, rattling stone for stone, parking parallel to Lidman's Ford. Upon Horse and Bird or rather thin and fashionable leaving the vehicle, dry malodorous smoke percolating the ice cold atmosphere attacks their pricey presents, its puffing point, a mustard painted motor, simultaneously mounted on a decorative bird bath and the splintered limb of a birch tree bent double.

Margo wrinkles her upper lip, disapprovingly.

"I recognise that yellow jalopy, belongs to Marian's little work friend, oh what's her name again?…Ethel, that's it, she gave me a ride home in that death machine once, her feet hardly reached the pedals, it was ridiculous, simply ridiculous, personally I find her a bit much."

"Well I can't think of any reason why a woman would need to drive, it's dangerous on the roads," said Ben, adjusting his designer overcoat.

Coughing smog under an apricot sky, they reach the heavy oak entrance, gratefully lit by the front doors hanging light. The precious gifts are bundled into Ben's handsome hooves as Margo ribbons her thin lips with a third coat of thick mahogany lipstick.

"Don't knock yet, I want to look my best."

Clairvoyant moths, hide behind the hanging lantern as the Wife's careful application is suddenly obtusely crooked due to a resonating, ghostly tenor voice calling out from behind the smoking motor.

"Can't fix it tonight Ethel! It's getting dark!..."

Deadly still on the stoop, unable to see anyone through the overcast bonfire haze emanating from the overheated engine grill, Margo sharply squawks into the chatty grim cloud.

"Who's there?!"

The cloud goes silent. Ben berates likewise.

"I say, who's there…speak up"

Slowly the figure of a man emerges out of the billowing white Sulphur, pleasantly smiling and carefully cleaning black oil from his fingertips with a grubby green handkerchief.

"Sorry folks! Thought you were Ethel," said the Stranger in a light, beguiling manner. "Said I'd give her engine a once over but unfortunately the drive belt's snapped, so it'll have to wait till tomorrow, no harm in trying though eh."

Gradually moving closer to their still stooperage, the Stranger reclothes himself with a fainted dinner jacket from an escorting forearm. Margo's inherent judgemental gaze takes in the cleanly shaved cleft chin, short curly black hair and two round sizeable ears either side of a square jaw, a touch of the Greek she thought, smartly turned out, olive mid thirties skin and finally his eyes, which although inviting and wide, she concluded to be of simple, commonplace, garden variety brown, an observation instantly changed by the telling glow of the hanging light, revealing his eyes to be something quite different entirely, as if shining to the back of two amber painted glass orbs delighted with curves of illuminated beige and bright pricks of mellow yellow and gold.

"I'll be honest with you," said the Stranger. "I'm quite relieved that I'm out here, she's hauled me along to this little gathering, but I don't really know anyone, I haven't even been in there yet, oh-h-h I'm sorry, I'm just chatting away with no introduction, how rude of me, the names Freddie…"

Holding out a relaxed friendly palm, the two males of similar six-foot height, firmly shake hands.

"Now that's a handshake with purpose, I've often found a good strong handshake is a telling sign of just how committed a man is. A trait of success, would you agree?" said Freddie, easy going and cool, devoting all his attention to Ben who's light suspicion quickly turns to a puffed out chest, responding in a fake baritone.

"Absolutely! As my father always says, all you need to be lucky in life is half a brain, expensive shoes and a dosh firm grip, although a big fat wallet doesn't do any harm!!!"

Cheerfully, the two males roar with laughter, a nippy Margo joining in with a sarcastic snort at her husband's crass wit.

"My name is Ben, 'B' 'E' 'N', Ben Barrister, if you're a cricketing man you may have heard of me, the last two years I've cracked wicket for Warwickshire, just as a Gentleman mind you, oh and this is the wife Margo." whinnied the Horse as Buzzard broods over her limp willy of an introduction.

"Well to meet you both is aces," said Freddie, winsomely. "I like your coat by the way Margo, sophisticated and powerful. So which fine folks do you know tonight?"

"Well, that's very kind of you to say, it's real mink. Just Marian and her Father and I know Ethel slightly, she's such fun to be with, I remember once she..."

Before Margo can finish, Freddie abruptly interrupts.

"Do you mind if we chin wag inside Margo, the weather's not on our side I'm afraid."

"Yes darling, stop keeping us chatting in this godawful chill bite!," cried Ben, rearing up to bang the brass knocker, five times in succession. "Let us in! We're god dog freezing!"

The deep faint movement of gorilla-ish footsteps approaches from inside, growing ever more pronounced until the sliding shutter gapes its fellatio yawn. The piercing incandescent sapphires of Daniel J. Lidman glow through the rectangle, growling in a boss office boom.

"Right! All of you listen up, I was going to ask you what the password is, but apparently it's no longer amusing to the guests who are already here, so to keep things interesting, we have decided to ask a ripping riddle, the one who comes up with the correct answer gets my last cigar, literally, now you can't say better than that can'ya!"

"Oh please, no games Mr. Lidman, it's practically the north pole out here, can't we just come in?" moaned Margo, inhaling with chattering teeth as the doorman declines.

"Nope! Not until you solve the riddle, those are my rules, and I'm telling my childhood favourite so you know it's a hard one, now then... what always runs but never walks, often murmurs but never talks, has a bed but never sleeps, has a mouth but never eats?"

"...Oh dear, I think we're going to freeze to death chaps," said the Horse, proceeded by a woolly headed Wifey.

"What was the first part again?"

The Stranger hanging back, casually admires how thick and immovable the heavy front door is, before allowing a lick of thinkage.

"Always runs, but never walks...it has a bed... it's a river!"

Lidman's blue jewels meet the amber gaze of the Greek. A crescent grin growing in the willow wood gap.

"You got it, well done clever egg, you've just saved yourself from a long, cold night, now everyone inside before you get frostbite on my property!"

"Did he get it? Bravo Freddo!"

Sliding back the panel, Daniel's handle hand moves to open the heavy oak entrance. Panicking, the front door jams its Suffolk latch, yank!-yank!-yank!, the lock begins to surrender and slip under the strain of its owner as the mud stained mat cries with wallowing whimpers to hold on just a few moments longer, but it's too late, clunk! The front door opens with a shameful creak as Margo, Ben and the newly introduced Freddie bundle their way in, shaking off the ravagement of nature's chill into the well heated kitchen that still has a faint trace of burnt pie about it.

Marian and Ethel rush from the living room, beaming with joy at the abundance of youth now injected into the party, pursued timidly by a disgruntled Larry, still recovering from Ethel's squeaking belief that the death penalty should be extended to anyone being boring in public places.

Snatching the gifts from hubby's possession, Margo presents them to birthday girl M, who barely contains her brimming girlishness, lovingly embracing store bought stuff and Buzzard in one slenderly armed Cat rap.

"Evening all Chaps! Happy Birthday, prezzies and all that!" projected Ben, dramatically whirling off his long coaterage with the live flamboyance of a mad matador as Wifey finally breathes from a feline squeeze.

"It's a painting set Mari, watercolours, hope that's OK and the cufflinks are for your Father."

Sniffing the Parejo shape of his last cigar, a counter leaning Lidman seemingly ignores the prospect of improving his cuffs, preferring to extend a beckoning finger towards Freddie's friendly and far away face.

"You, come here."

Standing for a brief moment, F surveys the elderly ape before strolling through the new sparks of party banter, to accept the weight of Daniel's hairy hand on his broad shoulder, jovial yet rough in its connection.

"Right here it is, my last... sorry whats'ya name lad?"

"My names Freddie, Mr. Lidman."

"Well Fred, this is my last Havana cigar, just look at it, isn't it beautiful and you won it fair and square, now listen up because this is important... I'm accustomed to smoking one a day, the Doc's

say I need to cut down or there'll be conse-
quences, so if I try and buy it back by the end of
the night, you refuse me flat, because above all
else I am a man of my word."

Briskly the last Havana is shoved into the
complete concealment of Fred's front pocket as
Ben's bronco tone, ping balls the kitchen walls.

"Who the bloody hell is Antoinette!?...I can't
survive on chocolate walnuts all night!"

"Yes you can, you haven't even tried yet," said
the Cat, prim Bird concurring with a lifted beak.

"Well I think it's a wonderful idea Mari, French
is it? I would have thought as much, they're so
cultured over there...unlike someone."

As the playful pretend argument develops
between good friends, Freddie senses the sizzling
worth of two solitary grey eyes, staring at him
from across the room, predicting its dessert table
position he confronts the sizzle just in time to
see Ethel's peering pupils dart back down to her
empty plate. Taking into account her age, height
and every clumsy mouse-like movement, the Greek
proceeds with lashings of likeability towards DL's
wine pouring counterage.

"Those cream scones do look delicious over there, do you mind if I try one?"

"Well since you're polite enough to ask, you eat as many as you can Lad, before they go stale."

Nodding respectfully, the placid Fred walks the far distance among mingling chatter to the spread of nectarous nibbles, standing opposite the bowed crown of E, her picky ponder popped by a table end question.

"It's Ethel isn't it?"

Ethel looks up.

"Oh hello, yes that's me...who are you? I mean, it's nice to meet you, what's your name?"

"My names Freddie and before you say it, yes I'm very much aware how silly a name it is, like a lost dog tag, I'm starting to think I should change it to something else."

"Freddie's good, it's bouncy, I like it" said E, fighting her inner anxiety at having to converse with yet another complete and total stranger.

"Well if you like it Ethel, that's all the persuasion I'd ever need to hold it dear all my life. I fixed it by the way."

"I'm sorry?"

"Your car outside, I fixed it...the drive belt was snapped, luckily I had a spare one in my glove compartment, you'll drive away like a dream now."

"I didn't know it was broken...Thank you, honestly though how much did it cost, I won't have anyone out of pocket because of me."

"I would never and could never take anything from you Ethel, let me have my good deed for the day."

Swaying shyly, hiding her slight tipsiness of two glasses of wine, Ethel's childish neck leans coyly to one side.

"...Are you a member of Marian's dads coin club thing? Please tell me you're not, you look far too alive for that."

"Good lord no, old things don't interest me, I like new things, for the simple reason that they never get old."

"Clever. Are you the neighbour's son then? Mrs. Betridge, is she still coming?"

The Greek's analysing amber calmly scans the guestly gaggle.

"...I'm sure she'll be here soon, you know how women of a certain age can be, they can never find anything to wear, Mother and I just live up the road, you know...I've passed this beautiful Cottage so, so, many times, it's a bit of a thrill to finally see what the inside looks li..."

A wet, gungey sound tenses the Greek, loud and lingering, the phlegmy clearance of a red roman nose.

Revolving carefully, F is fully confronted by a grumpy, cardigan mound of ginger weasel fuzz.

"I want to get to the biscuits, you're standing in front of them...makes it hard to get to them," said Larry with a further clearing of thick phlegm, causing Ethel to scarper off to join Marian's moulting conversation about moving to Paris to attend gourmet cookery classes.

With a step to the left, Larry creeps forward beside Fred and proceeds to fondle each individual biscuit, checking for discoloration.

"...Did I hear you say you were the neighbours son?"

"Sorry I didn't catch your name?" Fred retorted, thrusting a hand of friendship, receiving a limp bundle of flaccid fish fingers for a handshake.

"Larry...I work in a museum."

"Well Larry it's a pleasure to converse, so you and Mr. Lidman collect coins is that right?"

"Yes that's right, NCA member and proud of it, but I've known Daniel since nineteen fifteen or is it sixteen. He was my Captain at Whittington Local Defence during the War, he was a good Cap, stern but fair, some hard days back then, you know I sprained my ankle in a rabbit hole when we were patrolling a field in Polesworth, it happened three days before Christmas and I had to eat my turkey dinner with my foot up on a stool."

"Mr. Lidman's a Captain?...you've just made me very happy Larry."

Grinning away from the biscuit scented Ferret, Freddie surveys his weatherly watch for the first time.

"7.59pm."

At that precise moment a jolly contralto voice, sings to a high soprano outside the heavy oak entrance.

"Yooouwhoooo! It's meeee!"

The Birthday Boy lights up, lumbering latch way.

"Is that my favourite farm girl? I think it is."

"Father don't mess around with the shutter, just let the poor woman in, it's starting to rain again." said Marian, spotting the return of windy water lines, sprinting down the window glass.

Clunk! The front door swings its achingly slow hinges to a large, buxom, sixty-seven year old whale of a woman with two enormous bosoms matching the girth of her bulging stomach, a thick hessian handbag laying against her plentiful thighs that stretch and jiggle beneath a floral dress of deepest purple.

"Happy Birthday Daniel!" chanted the operatic woman, holding up a shimmering oval platter, covered with a chrome dome lid.

Lidman rows a welcoming log arm.

"Toddle'on in Mrs. Betridge, feel my warmth!"

Smiling inanely with an unruly grey mane, Betridge wobbles in like a violet hippo, purposely ponging of lady lavender to mask the pungent notes of wet manure embedded in her boots.

"Gre-e-etings you lovely dear people," she said, in a light breathy voice, almost woeful in tone. "I'm dreadfully late, I got caught up with one of my cows you see, she hasn't been able to express poor thing, but all she needed was a change of diet and a good firm hand and all that milk came squirting out like magic. Oh...I see you're already on the desserts, well if anyone's got hollow legs or otherwise hungry, I've whipped up a beef Wellington with leek and onion gravy for this grand occasion..."

Gleaming from ear to ear with sad soulful eyes, the wide hipped Hippo rises her shiny platter, creating an immediate surge of leaning interest.

"She's got food, real food!" said a wide eyed Horse.

"That looks very heavy, let me take that tray Mrs. Betridge." smiled Lidman licking his lips, taking the flat silver into his moulding monkey grip.

"Oh thank you, god bless a sweet man with manners, careful it's a bit hot."

"That really does smell good," said the Buzzard with Mouse and Ferret bobbing their bonnets in agreement.

Performing a theatrical peek under the chrome cover, DL straightens up with a silverback simmer, commanding the room with a sonorous grumble.

"Everyone! There is no point hiding the fact, that we now have a hot, nutritious meal in our possession, with leek and onion gravy, and as I speak and speak I do, it's getting colder and colder and there's no time to waste, so to all who hate the dentist, grab your glasses and follow me to the dining room!"

Marching out of the kitchen, platter in hand, deep into the bunting bliss, the Host passes the solitary staircase and takes a sharp right down the coffee coloured corridor followed by a tinkerling xylophone of wine glass melody and the giggling guff's of migrating party guest with a moody Marian leading the charge.

"H-a-ay! This was meant to be a Marie Antoinette themed party Dad, with cakes and buns."

"Don't worry sweetheart, the night is young and them sweets aren't going anywhere. Keep up everyone!"

Spellbound baited by the hearty smell of beef, the hungry posse moves together as one down the ebony brown hallway, encountering on their train line travels a sealed study and one dying wall light, flickering for help at the end of the aisle.

"I say chaps! Where are you taking us?" Said a berry bottle Horse, saddled with two under each arm.

Upon reaching the flicker flick flicker, another sharp right leads them down yet another narrow corridor of half the length. Waiting at ways end, eager for customers, two lonely stained glass doors lay lame with a hibernating hook latch holding them together.

Hook swung to a yawning hang, the full add of eight stroll between the colourful parted panes into a square and scarcely used dining room, scaling the respectable measurements of five meters in every direction, the majority of which taken up by a regal table of darkly varnished oval cedar and its neatly tucked offspring of ten chairs.

Dusty bulbs, glow burning with a dim lit romance, the Cat reluctantly raids a silverware sideboard for clean enough cutlery and sufficient fine china for every gluttonous guest.

Chromed and domed, the shimmer is placed at the foot of the table, wafting its perfection, the sexy sight of the beef wellington finally revealed by its lifted lid, an ear pricked Horse nudging a quite Fred with a wink of approval as everybody piles into their selected comforts.

"A sword, so I can vanquish this beast!" hollered Host, handed a small serrated bread knife. Sawing equal-ish slices, he distributes accordingly amongst the posh platerage.

"And now the gravy!"

Mrs. Betridge carefully unveils from her hessian handbag, a topped milk bottle, full of globby meat stock with various dismembered vegetables drowning around against the murky glass.

"Oh good it's still warm, do you mind if I serve it out, I simply love sloshing my gravy and there is a trick to it you know, not too little and not too much."

The Hippo proceeds to orbit her rotund radius around the chairs, proudly pouring out a precise amount from the recycled milk bottle.

"None for me, gravy makes me gassy," said the Ferret.

Crab stepping the tiny gap between chairs, the Betridge whale leans forward, pressing her gigantic farm filly breasts into Larry's bewildered rodent face, sloshing thick steaming gravy all over his reluctant plate.

"You're a growing male that needs nourishment, and there's nothing wrong with a man's potent gust, it's a sign of a good gut."

Reversing from Rat, Mrs. B rotates the table once more to meet her empty seat between Freddie and Ben.

"I think I'll squeeze amongst these two strapping Boys, I'm a lucky lady tonight," she said with a flirtatious titter.

Still stood at the cedar's foot, Lidman dominantly leans his fisted limbs onto the woodgrain.

"I have a speech and I'll keep it short, thank you all for coming, it's Marion's twenty-third and my sixty-fifth, still can't believe I'm that old...anyway, this day for me...is a date to be treasured, because on this very day twenty-three years ago, I got given the best gift that any man could ever ask for, I know that sounds soft...but old men grow soft for a reason, Happy Birthday sweetheart!"

Plodding his sweaty, wood log body to a sequin green happy Cat, the hairy Father kisses her young forehead to the clapping cheer of hip, hip hooray as cutlery clinks down to the slow cooked beef.

"So chaps! What do you think of Stanley Baldwin as Prime Minister? He'll never fill the bulldog's basket if you ask me," mumbled Ben with a mouth full of meat, assuring an inner irk from a temperamental Wife.

"Dear, I think we best stay away from politics."

"...Righto, well does anyone know any good jokes?!"

"I knew one once, it was about a frog that jumped off a cliff...or was it a toad," Larry droned, staring into space over the reply of a wine swill-ing DL.

"I've got one that's half bearable, it's a longy-long though."

"Oh, I just adore long jokes, they're like funny story's, oh go on tell it, tell it please," begged Betridge.

"Very well, top up your drinks and try not to split ya'sides...an Englishman is going off to the War, he hugs his wife and son and tells them he'll be back soon. Just as he's leaving, the son, little Jim, says 'daddy please bring me back a present' and the father says 'sure little Jim what would you like?' And the son says 'I want a German hel-met with a spike on top' and the father says 'I'll see what I can do' and within a week the Eng-lishman is in the thick of it, jumping in and out of trenches, dodging bullets, ducking shells the lot. He ends up in a very wet and very muddy ditch and would you believe it, there glinting in the mud is a German helmet, the Englishman thinks 'Oh what luck, I'm having that for little Jim' so he grabs the helmet by the spike and pulls,..it doesn't budge an inch, so he gets a good footing and with two hands he pulls, and pulls and pulls until suddenly he hears someone gasping for air under the helmet, 'bloody hell, there's a German attached' thought the Englishman, and the German says...I can't do the accent but I'll try anyway, 'Please don't kill me Tommy, I'vant to live..."

Adjusting his volume slightly over the meat porcelain rhythm of tink-tink-tink, the Host hammers on.

"And the Englishman says! 'Hello German, I see you've got yourself stuck in the mud' and the German replies 'yar, yar, mud me stuck, yes Tommy' 'If I pull you out of the mud can I have your helmet to give to my son little Jim' says the Englishman. 'Yar, yar little Jimmy yar! Sure Tommy, you pull, you pull!' So, the Englishman pulls with all his might, with every bit of strength he has and after half an hour the German is still buried up to his armpits, 'I can't seem to pull you out of the mud' says the exhausted Englishman, and the German says 'V'ould it help if I took my feet out of the stirrups!'"

Resounding in chorus, a guestly groan echoes the dimly lit dining room.

"That was bloody awful! Worse than one of mine and my jokes are unbearable!" laughed the Horse, officially semi-drunk.

As the plentiful wine continues to flow, the chatter picks up over the communal tune of eating, pollinated with individual group grabbles; Betridge happily telling Freddie and Ben about her addition to knitting as the three gossiping girls reveal all they know about flirtatious film stars and the hell bent harlots of hot Hollywood.

Patting his old stomach at the successful table talk, Daniel leans back in his chair to correspond with a wilted Chum, still unsuccessfully trying to scrape a sea of gravy off his bathing beef.

"Quite a nice turn out Larry."

"Yes..people."

"...I'm glad Mrs. Betridge's son decided to give it a miss, otherwise the portions would have been even smaller."

Larry sniffs and licks a dabbed digit of brown onion juice, in a moment of silence before replying.

"...That black haired man's her son, he was in the way of the biscuits."

"The clever egg?...Oh good, so there was enough to go around, that's a full house then," smiled Lidman, leisurely catching the elderly eye of Betridge from across the dining crossfire, lifting his drink to the happy mum and son as they both raise their glasses in kind.

Stacked one by one with left over gravy and gristle, the pasted plates are gathered together for fear of slowing down the last dizzy bottle of Spanish Merlot, circulating the oval rim, eventually ending up in the Greeks possession.

"Mrs. Betridge, there are three things in a woman's life that should never be empty, her heart, bed and glass, may I refresh it for you?"

"No, no not for me you kind boy, I've only just finished my last one, I'm not used to drinking like this you know, I'm starting to feel tiddly," said the Hippo, fluttering her grey lashes at the gliding surface of Fred's clever knee, grazing the outside of her gigantic thigh, making a delicate friction between wild wool and thin purple.

Uncontrollably blushing the whale woman begins giggling like a giddy schoolgirl.

"Oh go on then! Just a small one mind."

Plucking her glassy stork, F steadily pours the old world red waiting for her to halt the flow, only ceased by common sense and Mrs. B's impression of a snorting walrus.

"Easy up there or I'll be anyone's by the end!"

Hurling a hearty guffaw, she clamps her faint lady mustache around the glass, taking a large gulp of fresh Merlot. Sinking slightly in the creaking chair, she looks at Freddie with a sad slinky smile of intoxication.

"Oh you're a good lad you are ain't ya, he's a good lad he is!" she said, telling anyone around the table who would listen.

Fulfilling the role of hostess, Marian floats to her feet, lifting the pile of plates.

"I'll just quickly wash these up, one less thing to worry about, any helping hands...Margo?.. Ethel?"

Hearing their names called in such a matter of fact tone, Buzz and Mouse dutifully stand with agreeable attendance for the slender M.

"I'll take the plates, Margo the cutlery please and Ethel grab that platter, we can't let Mrs. Betridge take it home like that..."

Joining her long stride, the three young fem's pass the rainbow glass, disappearing up the coffee coloured corridor.

Predicting a sudden lull due to the lack of young lady's, Ben proceeds to rock his chair back and forth, thinking of new hilarities.

"I say...I say Mr. Lidman, I noticed you have a piano in the living room, mind if I blow the dust off and give it a whirl? I only know Greensleeves but it's not a real party without a sing song."

"If you must," said DL, folding his furry forearms. "It'll be good to see that old relic put back to work."

Up and unseated, the Horse canters on the spot.

"How about it Freddo, fancy turning the pages for me?"

"...I'd be delighted, if you will excuse me Mrs. Betridge, I must turn another man's pages."

"Yes, you boys run along and have fun, you leave us oldy's to put our feet up," said the Hippo with a simmering smug mug as Lidman winces at the prospect of being called an 'oldy'.

The two males march out of the dining room in the way of the women, minus the grace and gowns, leaving the three elders to their worldly wisdom.

Investing a Pot-Bellied grunt, Daniel eyeballs the empty chairs, the empty bottles on the table.

"Look at all those dead soldiers Corporal, it's quite a sight isn't it..."

Nodding, the Ferret grows nostalgic for the regiment days of 'do this, do that'.

"Yes Captain, they're all empty...want me to fetch more?"

"I'm afraid as far as wine is concerned, they've all bought it, the very last drops of bravery, lay solely in that fair lady's glass over there...how do they taste Mrs. Betridge?!"

"...Sweet and brave" she said with an accidental burp.

Sitting bolt upright, the Host blue darts around the middle distance with a thinking frown.

"Hang on a second...there is another bottle, behind the stove."

Hippo raises one eyebrow.

"Stove?"

"Yes, I put it there last week because my uncle Basil had his heart broken by a Hungarian girl when he was sixteen."

Hippo raises two eyebrows.

"I don't understand Daniel...does he have a drinking problem?"

"No, I forgot to mention he was visiting, I hid the bottle because the wine's made in Hungary, the smallest hint of anything Hungarian and he bursts out blubbing, but the point is we're back in business, Larry! In the kitchen behind the Rayburn stove, get out there and bring our man home safely."

"Understood Captain!"

Larry fusses up with a limp wristed salute, creeping out of the dining square to the din of Ben's butchered rendition of Greensleeves, playing down the corridor.

Moving in turn to sit creak another chair, the farm filly closes the gap between her and Host to a whispering intimacy.

"I must say neighbour, I'm having the most wonderful time, thank you so much for inviting us."

Content, Daniel mini waves a discouraging hand.

"Now I won't hear that, the pleasure is all mine and I want you to know, that you are welcome at this Cottage anytime you like, Fred as well, he's a clever lad."

"Oh, most definitely, you know he's been teaching me about a new way to knit my woolen tea cosies, it's a cross stitch with a three centimetre dip down, it will save me a ton of yarn if I can master it, but everybody has been so lovely tonight and it looks like my beef wellington went down a treat, thank goodness I cooked a large one'eh."

Before Daniel can coin a complement, her expression turns strangely sombre.

"Shame about George though, he really wanted to come tonight, he's attending a three day conference in Doncaster, it's terrible having him away from home, even for a few days, but if it helps him get that promotion in Brum, then full steam ahead I say..."

Lidman's primitive rock face, crease leans politely with two perplex twinkles newly glinting under, above and all around a bed of wrinkles.

"...I'm sorry who?"

Mrs. B sets off giggling again, playfully paw patting his shoulder.

"You kidder, you know my George, he drives past almost everyday on the way to work, he said he saw you gardening last week, I didn't know you had a green thumb, we should share potting tips sometime."

Oddly still, Lidman looks away from her.

"...George...George is your son?"

"Yes silly, you sent us an invite last month... don't you remember?"

Quiet blues gliding ray-like along the whirling woodgrain of the table, a cold slither wriggles down Daniel.

"...How many sons do you have Mrs. Betridge?"

"Oh Just the one, plenty enough for a widow, George was a real hand full when he was a youngen, you couldn't keep your eyes off him for one second without him banging into something."

Hunching his bell tower shoulders into an uncomfortable stoop, the Boss aggressively rubs the bumpy rough meat of his temple and cheeks.

Betridge taps his hairy table arm.

"...Everything alright Dear? You've gone awfully pale...It's not my food is it? Oh I just knew I should have left it in longer!"

Turning his bull neck to a worried Whale, Lidman creases up his entire face into a counterfeit grin.

"I suddenly feel an overwhelming urge to join the others for a sing song."

"...Oh yes lets; we'll show them we still have some spirit left in us, although, a young ticket should never be envied Daniel, they queue for the bus the same as us."

Creaking their heavy bones from a fading comfort, they escort each other passed the multicoloured glass, changing to black in Lidman severity.

Navigating the pecan passageway, its lengthy walls suspect. The amateur abundance of wrong keys abruptly stops.

Silence.

As if strangled back in tune, the screaming sound of a petrified piano, plays back up again but with one fundamental difference, the ham fisted, school boy playing has been replaced; replaced by the fast running, ghostly tempo of Ragtime Blues, never yet heard by English eardrums and only ever played, let alone listened to, in the deepest, darkest corners of down town Louisiana, the alley black scream of New Orleans.

CHAPTER FOUR:

The Room

Swarming from devilish key fingers, the flying nimble notes, rag their bone rhythm
down the coffee coloured corridor to greet
with grave animosity, the sinewy shoulders of a
stampeding Lidman, glare bulbing the return of
Larry and bottle with an echoing succession of
booming grunts.

"Go back Larry! We're joining Ben's sing
song..."

"Yes!, We're pulling up our socks and joining
the young," huffed a breathy Betridge, struggling
to keep up.

"Oh, I'll go with you then shall I?" Replied the Ferret, turning back with a slight stumble.

"The smiling bloke is not the one playing though, that angry little girl booted him off the stool because he wasn't very good at playing piano."

Crossing a deceased wall light and study, the elders finally advance out of the long dong espresso into the bright bunting bliss, their dilating peeps titillated by four sets of swaying legs, dancing in small scuffles around the grand piano, tapping their young toe-toes to the strange music.

"It's awfully fast isn't it?!" smiled Betridge, wobbling on to join and jive the whirling semi-circle.

Treading behind, striking a sad shape with a pronounced bottom lip, a frowning, belly green Boss sidles likewise to the rabble of melody minded guests. A fluctuating gap between the two merry M's, showcasing a talented question mark, the grim, soulful spectre of an intently playing Freddie.

Riddled with red ambivalence, the unbearable need to point, the need to shout, interrogate in front of everyone is abruptly interrupted by Larry's cuddling waiterage of an ugly yellow bottle, held babyish against his brown buff with stroking rat nails.

"Needs a corkscrew Captain..."

"Is that the last bottle? There's an opener in the kitchen," said a threshold bounding Marian, thirsty and eager to renew the sudden dry drought.

Taking the opportunity to not be corrected by a homely Daughter, Lidman steals closer to the grand piano with a falling haze brain, the relentless ragtime haunting his every second as he tries to be, in a word, tactful.

"Come to think of it!, there's plenty of wine!" exclaimed the old man over the loud music, dazed and blinking with no care of coherence. "Lots and lots of it, a case of it in my study, it's quite a big case, heavy, I'll need some help bringing it out!"

Dotting the end of a hostly tone, Fred immediately stops playing and lowers the bruised and crying fall board over a tired row of violated keys.

"I'll help!" said Ben, flexing his cricket muscles for comic effect.

"No, no Lad, I remember you brought bottles to the dining room, you've done your bit...it's Fred's turn."

Lidman waits for a presumable 'Yes I'd love to help' from an always cordial Freddie, but in lieu of this without saying a word, he stands and steps away from the school boy stool and waits in turn with a soft wry smile.

Perpetually beetle browed, Lidman commands with a directional fist to follow him.

"Down here lad, won't take long..."

Groaning at the loss of their talented player, the amber eyed man is escorted away from the rest of the guests and back down the lengthy brown corridor to the locked study, which to Lidman's touch opens without needing a key, this equates the impossible to an incontinent strike plate and DL knowing a precise wrist jiggle.

"Guest's first..."

Relaxed and cool, Freddie strolls through a frame of stale air into a dark cerebellum grey room with no windows or ventilation of any kind, the longish floor plan dominated by erect filing cabinets, sprouting from the ground like ambitious tree trunks, their dumb-dumb corners casting fat duvet shadows across shaded items of miscellaneous meaning, a spare chair with a broken seat, a fist cracked wall mirror propped against an old rocking horse, left over from Marion's childhood.

Standing in the middle clearing, overcast and grim, the lurid Greek ignores the surrounding features as DL locks the door behind them, snap goes the latch, their minuscule room movements made ever more pronounced by the runty reverberation of oblivious party guests laughing down the way.

Hiding his nature, the Host turns with a fake lightheartedness.

"S-o-o-o Fred...thank you for helping...you told me your name was Fred,..and you're...Mrs. Betridge's son, is that right?..."

Not responding, the well postured Freddie remains eerily unaffected, like a well crafted waxwork, never talking, never moving, always smiling slightly.

Sapphires glinting in an oversized skull, the brutish cross boss grinds his old grey chompers, proceeding to the next unavoidable question.

"...This party, who invited you?"

Noir in mood, the room resonates in the ensuing silence. Smile fading away in olive skin shadow and pools of haze grey light, the square jawed genie replies matter of factly.

"Nobody Mr. Lidman..."

"...Lad!...I'm about to get really, really angry, so you be right careful now...I know you haven't come with Larry, you're not Mrs. Betridge's Son... so you're one of Ben's friends are you? And you're a jokester, you like jokes..."

"...A tad under two hours Mr. Lidman, that's how long I've known your guests," said the Greek, with a queer lick of pride.

Suffering a familiar chest pain, the old man rises red, with a spit clenching pressure bursting through a hateful vibration.

"You've just walked in? In off the street! Into my home...you better start telling me who you are Lad, something for the police!..."

Freddie winces with equal irritation.

"I'm not from the street Mr. Lidman...and I could tell you all about me but it doesn't really matter, I will however tell you that the reason for me being in your delightful home is what you might call a 'business matter'. I've been approached by a company, a local company, that has expressed a great deal of interest in your work affairs and given your refusal to sell, have calculated my services as being a far more cost effective way for them to proclaim ownership of said business, now the good news Mr. Lidman,...it has been brought to my attention and you should thank your last bit of luck that it was...you have not yet stated in your will, that the list of zero living beneficiaries of Lidman and Son Accountancy, includes one 'Marian Elizabeth Lidman', although I'm sure you were planning on doing so very soon, you should see your neglect in these matters as a spot of good fortune considering the circumstances."

Flustered by the barrage of speech, Lidman sharp barks in bafflement.

"Local company!...What are you talking about?"

"You haven't been listening to a word I have been saying have you Mr. Lidman, I've been hired to murder you."

A rosy river drains from DL, leaving a white sheeted man, the cold hospital distilled fear boiled back in an instant by an altogether new river of black anger.

"...You're going to kill me boy?, you've walked into my home, without being invited, and you think 'You' are going to kill 'Me'."

Intruder engulfed by a Gorilla man shadow, Lidman seems to double in size by aid of good posture, channelling his inner brute from thirty years ago, his huffing barrel chest causing a fat bottom lip to stick out more than ever, a bright red cushion bedding the crazed glint of Saliva covered ivory as a peaceful Greek sails a slender hiss across the hot minded study.

"If it came to that, I think it would be a very messy outcome for both of us, but fortunately I don't prepare for bare knuckle boxing for each employment, use your imagination or better yet your riddling skills...noisy, made of metal and about my person at this very moment."

Joining the sounds of heart and huff, the irregular clip clap of drunken footsteps coming down the brown towards the locked study door reaches their mid attention. Calm and centralised, the Greek stares with half doll eyes at the soon to be rattled copper knob.

"...Don't unlock the door Mr. Lidman, they will automatically become my business as well."

Upon the falling thud of those fatal words, a fatherly fear swirls within Daniel, recognising the feline steps to be the very distinct movements of his own blood and love Daughter, a Daughter that shares with him all the knowledge of the household, including the jiggle.

Traveller stops. The handle rattles for a hot second before swinging into a door bound Lidman, stopping its fulfilment at a hinged pie slice.

"Hello Dad!" slurred a merry Marian, illuminating the gap.

Embedding scared nails into a painful frame, Lidman confronts his executioners mild surprise, unprepared for a failing lock. The pushing Cat opens the door fully to a boyish smile, clown painted across Freddie's shuddering jawline.

Excited, M pulls a pale DL into the hallway, sustaining her sloppy speech. "It's amazing and wonderful!, and, and beautiful and everything! Ben's brought champagne, real champagne! Quick, quick before it's all gone!"

Releasing a sweaty wet shirt arm, she glides away back up the coffee dong, disappearing into the far reaching bunt. Newly framed and un-changed, Fred proceeds with a deadly severity.

"Step back inside Mr. Lidman..."

"No, no you can't do this," whispered the Fa-ther, feverishly. "I don't know anyone who would hire you, I just run an accountancy firm, tax re-turns and rebate slips, that's all, that's all I do..."

"Tax returns?" Puzzled F, stepping the spine-like aisle.

"Yes, just a few small businesses, we take care of their books, that's it"

"...Small businesses? The baker and the toy shop on the corner, things like that?"

"Yes Lad, exactly, exactly like that"

"...There must be some mistake, I can't im-agine my employer would instigate a crime for such a minuscule operation such as that...well I suppose I better leave then."

The Greek lifts a thick black pair of Mediterranean eyebrows to the stress filled face in front of him.

"...Sarcasm boy," scowled Daniel with a sniffing grunt.

Fred moves closer with a twitch of annoyance.

"Must I really inject perspective...they have absolutely no interest in what goes on within the walls of Lidman and Son Accountancy...it's the building Mr. Lidman, and the ground that it stands on, which you solely own, just you, 'you'."

Old muscles beginning to crack and crumble, clenching, hot and heavy.

"...I can't believe this, why...why did you have to do this on my Birthday, our Birthday!"

"Mr. Lidman, I really can't stress enough the utter rarity of this conversation...you see I no longer complete a brief in front of their children, I've deemed it counterproductive, it really does mess with their little minds for pretty much their entire existence, but the real question is,

why are you alive 'now'. I've had a strange reve-
lation, would you like to know what it is, I think
you're going to like it very much. As a rule I would
have made it quick but the complication of there
being multiple people here has made it difficult,
now that is down to my foolish mistakes and not
yours, so given the climate of which I have already stated, I'm going to make you a deal."

"A deal? What is it, anything…"

Ever telling, the watch that hugs an olive arm
is checked for a second time.

"8:59pm. The deal is this, we head back to
the party, have a jolly old time with your family
and friends, drink as much as you want, eat as
much as you want, and at the end of the night,
when everyone has gone home or in your Daughter's case, gone to sleep upstairs, then we will find
a secluded quiet spot outside, most likely the end
of a field, and then…we will simply conclude our
business. This is my gift to you Mr. Lidman…
Happy Birthday."

Turning ghoulish and green, Daniel dribbles
a fractured plead.

"Please...you can't...don't!"

"The only other direction, return to the study, if you would rather not postpone the act any further."

Growing weaker by the second, the old man begins to hysterically admit a stop and start ghostly monotone moan of guttural giggling, rocking from his panicking larynx.

Quick as a quip, Freddie grabs two soft paddles of chesty fabric, pinning Lidman's rattle ban shoulders to the corridor wall to prevent him from collapsing into a crying heap.

"Listen to me very carefully," Freddie hissed. "Your body is trying to shut down, if it succeeds it will become impossible for me to offer you this very generous gift, to accept the changes and carry on as normal, a shock to the system is needed, I'm going to have to hurt you," the Greek viciously clamp's an unnaturally strong hand around Lidman's bumbling chin bunching up his jowly cheeks.

"I think I'll aim for the temple following your hair line, which will be for the most part invisible to the others, now given your natural temperament this should give you a good surge of rage, over-coming by force this unhelpful hysteria, blink three times if you would like me to continue."

Before Daniel's dead end lids, can shut out the light, a rough workman's hand crashes into his elderly pain-late nerve endings. Left to fall to the floor with an apish roar, the rabid Host pounds a hairy fist into the dusty dong, now feeling an endless elevator of pain.

"You're a Monster!..."

"Business only, a straight forward redundancy, you of all people should understand that. Now before we make our way back, let me state a warning to you as clearly as I can. I am at this present moment carrying a firearm as I'm sure you have already guessed, and I will be using it by the end of the night, I promise you that. Now you may take comfort in the fact, that the last thing I want is to murder an old man in front of his loved ones, but rest assured if you tell anyone who I am, or take advantage of my very painful present in any way, I will take no hesitation in fulfilling my docket then and there, and by the time the screams have stopped and help has arrived, I will be long gone, and so will you..."

With use of pale hand and hard wall, Lidman raises himself to a new found stability, silently nod signing the venomous verbal contract to Freddie's immense pleasure.

"Wonderful, now I think we both fancy another one of those delicious cream scones don't we... with plenty of butter."

Being made to walk in front in his own home, the lengthy sombre aisle, grows longer and longer in the maddening mind of old man D, watching the bright raised merriment unfold in a far living room with a galloping Ben showing off the champagne bottled beauty to a pair of gramophone ladies, a comfortably sitting Whale, a teetotal Ferret, finishing up at a barely drunk buzzard.

"Bosh to the wine chaps! I have the real thing!" promoted the Horse like a miracle man, boasting an all in one elixir to the moody re-emergence of Lidman's private crumble.

"Back of the car, forgot I had it!" smiled Ben, zealously. "Left over from a triumphant victory at Bournville, we were down by two wickets but right at the last their Anchor went belly up because of a backfired salmon bap and we whipped their bollards by seventy-nine runs!"

"Is this really from France or the knock off stuff we have at the Queens?" smirked Ethel, sparking a Stallion outrage.

"How dare you! Benjo only wins the best, genuine stock, this is made by the frogs and no mistake, you can tell by the shape of the bubbles."

Ben eye examines its green glass circumference, noticing a tall, bubbly Greek on the other side.

"Grand tour over then Freddie? Just be thankful he didn't show you his coin collection upstairs, a man would definitely need a good stiff drink after seeing a two hundred year old Spanish Nobbler."

"It's pronounced Ninckler," said Larry, rather put out.

"Hey! What did I say Larry, any more boring coin talk from you equals no glass of froggy juice."

"I told you I don't drink!" frowned the Ferret, nursing a glass of apple water.

"...Coin collecting isn't for everyone, it's an acquired skill, doesn't come easy to most people," retorted Lidman, trying his very best to perform a fake normality to Ben's high vibrancy.

"Well speaking of easy, we've just been playing a brand new parlour game I invented and this lot are easier to beat then a tambourine."

"That's because you cheated, I demand a rematch!" squeaked the Mouse, her squinting greys burning into the Horses hide as Betridge happy honks with nude perplexity.

"Oh yes lets, give it another whirl, I'm not sure I understood the first time."

Projecting, the wild Steed flicks a chestnut mane.

"It's a simple game Chaps! Even a monkey could figure it out, the name's 'Movie Star Magic!' We all choose a film star, don't tell anyone, don't give any clues, if you are picked by me, you have to stand by the fireplace and do an impression of your film star without using any sound and we have to guess who it is, but here's where it gets spicy! I also get to choose the only person who is allowed to guess, so everyone take a seat...let's start with the birthday girl with Larry to guess."

Avoiding a painful connection between blue and aiming amber, Daniel grouches a near comfort in his large leather throne while Monster cool steps to grace a more modest grandfather chair.

"I've got it, I've got someone in my head!" said Marian, pussy pouncing to the fireside clearing, immediately shooing off a flock of imaginary seagulls.

Correcting his freakishly magnified spectacles, Larry tweaks a puzzled pout as the girls bob in their noisy seat cushions aching to cry out the answer.

"Come on man, think! Who could it be? Just think," brashed Ben, encouragingly; a Cat's miming patients ebbing away as the stupefied, peer pressure Ferret bumbles a long groaning guess.

"Uuuuu Cha-a-arly Cha-a-aplin?"

"Mari is it Chappers!?" said the Horse, swinging a dramatic finger as Marian explodes out of her muteness with furious disbelief.

"Charlie Chaplin! How is this Chaplin!?"

She repeats the manic motion.

"It was obviously Arbuckle!"

Anxious, the grump gulps his shaking glass of apple before defending himself over the bunting room titters of 'yes I thought it was' and 'how did he not get that, the fool'.

"I don't really watch the flickers, can I pick a politician instead?"

"I'm the one who picks! You...man!" fumed an ever polite Marian; a soothing Stallion quickly redirecting the well watered players.

"Right, well that was a complete disaster. who wants to go next?..."

"May I have a go, I know just who to do, she's so sweet," said the Hippo, wobbling her way to the fireplace stage, a smiling Ben muting her rippling sing.

"Don't give us any clues Mrs. Betridge! Just give us your great impression, Margo to guess."

Lifting a giggle dress hem, the fat Lass curls her tattered grey hair into temporary ringlets around a pudgy finger, flirtatiously kissing the ambient air repeatedly in every direction.

"...Well I'm nonplus, venture a guess Darling?" shrugged the Horse to a prim Buzzard hiding her quiet queasiness brought on by the Hippo's oscillating farm flab.

"She's acting like a little girl, and curling her hair a lot...so my guess i-i-i-s...Pickford?"

Elated and loud, the nodding hippopotamus opera's insanely.

"Yes!, yes it was! It was Mary Pickford, does that mean I've won?..."

"It sure does Mrs. Betridge, I announce you the winner!" said Ben, clapping kindly.

Beaming with mad happiness, Betridge begins to bounce her large, elephant bosomed body, up and down on the red ruby carpet, overwhelmed with euphoric pleasure.

"I've won! I can't believe it, I've never won anything, oh the joy!"

Leaping her heavy belly once more in front of everyone, the wailing widow's skin briskly turns the colour of moldy white bread, still suspended in flight by a matter of milliseconds she collapses down to the ground with a godless thud, her vision dancing away in the big abyss, leaving only the tin tone sound of gasping girls and booming boys making indistinct statements like 'What's happened, are you ok Mrs. Betridge' and 'Quick!, get her off the floor for God's sake'.

With the exception of an unfazed Fred and a mortified Host, all in a mass they horizontally wrestle her groaning, dead weight onto the deep blue Chaise Lounge.

"What...what, where am I?" Whale whinged in a thin wafer of consciousness, creasing a pitiful brow at the concern creatures looking down at her.

"You fell down, made a very loud bang and now my ears hurt," remarked Larry, receiving evil red from every angle.

"Have I? Oh how very embarrassing, I'll see myself home" whimpered Mrs. B, close to tears, trying to replant her weak jelly legs.

"You can't walk home like this, just rest a moment," said Marian, leaning sweetly to brush plastered grey from a sweaty Hippo face.

"...Maybe you're right Dear, I suddenly feel incredibly sleepy, I can't seem to keep my eyes open, it's so strange, I think I'm..."

Falling into a deep slumber, the tonnage of her thick legs, thick arms, thick everything, settles still on the rich blue padding.

"Poor old biddy! Maybe she's had a bit too much to drink, she was rather putting it away earlier," mentioned the Horse, arms akimbo.

"Maybe let her sleep it off, what do you think Father?"

Clearing a painfully dry throat, DL grunts in agreement.

"Sleeping, yes...a glass of water, for when she wakes..."

Lidman nervously log steps his way into the kitchen, sensing the follow of the Greek's gradual shadow. Upon the threshold, DL steals to the sink feeling sick, flushing the taps cold splash over his steaming hot rock, drinking its country flow with a pooling monkey paw, the resembling desperation of a dying desert man finally reaching his oasis. With a drip drop sulk, he twist heels to a relaxed F, pillared on the centre tiles.

"She's collapsed?"

"Yes she has Mr. Lidman, how very observant of you, I think she may need cooling..."

Taking a near tea towel, Fred folds it up into a neat square and sails sink way to rinse its flowery middle.

Still glistening, Host suffers on the spot.

"Have you done this? What have you done to her? She didn't do anything wrong...I didn't do anything wrong."

"Calm yourself, it's just a mild sleeping draft, that's all. Slipped in her drink during the German joke. Given her size, I expect she'll be out for a good few hours."

"But why?..."

The Greek wrings the rag over the sink.

"Isn't it obvious, I did this for you, I thought you'd be happy."

"...Happy? Why in God's name would I be happy about this..."

Freddie's amber flashes with a twinkling temper.

"You're testing my patience...when there's so many other wonderful things you could be testing, use that abnormal brain of yours and think, who gave you knowledge of me. We can't have her plodding around, telling everyone how much she misses her son, but now you need not worry, you can enjoy your remaining birthday without fear of it being cut short by loose talk. Now,..I highly recommend you return to your party Mr. Lidman, before my prepared square becomes any dryer."

CHAPTER FIVE:

Soft Cushions

Low lit by two lamps, the cosy cohabitation settles in the embryonic bunt, the big bay frightfully framing a flirtatious night time reunion between Mr. Rain and the Wild Wind.

Minus a decomposing dead fox and a dozen brave wine bottles, the first casualty of the evening has now fallen. Beautifully grotesque in the corner of the room, the exhibit of Mrs. Betridge, spread eagled across the deep blue Chaise Lounge admitting the odd snore and groan from beneath a filtering damp rag is reluctantly endured in the party's new reflective ambience and newly still for good reason. Despite everyone's best efforts at precisely ten past ten, seated in a semicircle around a warm fireside, the pealing, crepuscular subject has finally approached and reared its ugly fresh head of remembrance, the remembrance of the War.

"I still can't believe it, to just drop like that, I've never seen anything like it," said Marian, pouring the Hungarian swill.

"I have," replied Larry proudly. "Old Bob in Burntwood, a hot Tuesday it was, we were building a wall outside the tree and sparrow pub, the heat got to him and poof! Down like a Welsh town, remember Captain?..."

The vermilion Ferret draws group attention to a sallow seated Daniel, surviving his second hour of internal torment.

"I didn't know you were a Captain Mr. Lidman?" queried Margo, maintaining a strict sitting posture.

"...Yes, served at Whittington barracks since I was a young man, when war broke, my rank was progressed to train local defence," Boss muttered meekly; amber gaze burning into his sad bubby blues as the red Rat continues his nook of nostalgia.

"Out of bed, seven-thirty each and every morning, a long jog, breakfast, and then we would learn how to spot the Hun a mile off, no matter what they were wearing..."

"That sounds cushy, really cushy and a lot easier than what me and Marian were put to work doing, three years in a munitions factory making shell cases, rifle butt's, leather pouches and two terrible months making fabric shrouds, big ones and small ones." Said the Buzzard, Horse holding her taloned hand with a loving husband hoof.

"You know darling, I've never asked you what that was like, the factory."

"...Well it was a lot of things, but in the main it was just hot, very, very hot. Sweat and grease would sting your eyes, everyone learnt the head handkerchief trick, day one."

Rolled by a reminiscing image, Marian cracks up with glee and laughter, releasing Margo's maximum humour capacity, a quiet breathy snigger.

"I know what you're thinking about."

Inquisitive, Ben grins with a pearly chomp.

"What's the gag gal's?"

Pointing at Margo, Marian tries to find her breath, calling out a single word through a cheery chuckle.

"Skunks!"

The Buzz smugly concurs in a girlish telepathy, not open to Ethel's impatient frown pout.

"Who or what is Skunks?.."

Simmering in fair memory, the kitty Cat proceeds with a playful tale.

"Skunks was the nickname we gave to one of the factory managers, he was pretty awful, treated us like dogs most of the time, but my he made us laugh, unintentionally that is, you see, although he was a complete tyrant, he was only Ethel's height, had a horseshoe mustache and a thick Newcastle accent, always shouting as well, always, the littlest things would set him off."

"I'm not that short!...Why Skunks?" Mouse interrupted.

"Yes Ethel I'm getting to that. Everyday he'd march on to the factory floor wearing a very unconvincing black toupee on his head and all his remaining white hair on the sides he would darken with shoe polish, it was basically painted on, but we could always tell when the heat raised up the blacking would mix with his sweat and melt down the back of his neck, I feel quite bad thinking about it, the amount of times I almost told him and then he would shout at me and I'd think well...never mind you angry little man, but the name 'Skunks' started when the rationing began and he couldn't get his hands on anymore shoe polish but he still kept coming in wearing that hair piece, a jet black hair piece, it was like looking at a chess board, and then one day Margo said 'he looks like a skunk' and it just caught on...I wonder where old Skunks is right now?..."

"Probably runs a shoe shine stand," said Ethel, her quick quip causing a prim Margo to simultaneously howl with virgin laughter while palming her loud brown beak with embarrassment.

"...And what of yourself Ethel, during the War?" inquired a smooth Greek, fixing mellow yellow to a childlike E, scratching a high neck itch beneath her red ruby headscarf.

"Me? I was a kid, Smithwick Elementary. We were evacuated to rural areas, ever seen one of them gloomy pictures with name tag kiddies at the station, that was me, I ended up on a farm in the far north, just outside a little village called Darlington, but I always pronounced it Ducklington. Anyway, I'd love to say I was part of some mucky dungaree wearing gang of close knit friends that had to band together to overthrow some wicked, slave driving farm owner, but the truth is, I was completely on my own, the whole time I was there no other children were dropped off, mind you it was only a small set up, just a brick farmhouse, a couple of chicken coops and a few cows and sheep and the odd postman, I lived with Mr. and Mrs. Blooms, they were both in their seventies and they weren't mean or cruel, they treated me like their very own daughter, it was safe, quiet and mind meltingly dull. Spent most of my time running around the fields with an old Spaniel called Bonzo, he was light brown...

I know how long dogs live, but I still like to think he's there now, still barking at the cow shed..."

Ethel goes quiet, drinking the last of her clasped wine glass with two tiny hands.

"Ben?" said Fred, softly addressing the drunk Stallion, straightening up at the bell of his name.

"South Staffordshire Regiment! Proud as I live and breathe Freddo! They used to call us 'the Staffys', we thought we were so tough, they had us all around the edges building coastal defences. I spent most of the War digging, very, very long, very, very deep ditches in case the German's had us on the run, and we thought that was going to be it for us, but then six months before every-thing ended the field Marshal shipped us to froggy land just a few miles from the front, the shovels became guns and our lot was thrown in with the Scotties and told to grow a stiff lip if we didn't want a fat lip."

Ben's buoyant demeanour slips to a sad physicality.

"...Three months we were there, we inter-cepted the German's six times, lost one of my mates on a Monday, hard day that, I can't recall much but I do remember thinking...this is the longest day I've ever lived, but there we are, hay-ho and all that..."

Low in his throne more frown than face, Daniel spots a slight change in Freddie's marigold holes, a respectful twinkle, a weakness of honour, observed not only by him but also Ethel, spinning her question canon to a far seated Greek.

"And what about you?, let me guess, you were a fighter pilot, flying high above the clouds, shooting down the cross and spying on German warships over the Pacific"

"...Not quite," said the Monster. "I was a military man before the War, we were stationed in South Africa for a good few years, protection for British colonies, and then Swaziland for two and then come the 13th of May 1915, we were sent across the world to the north side of a very beautiful French river, with very beautiful green trees and very beautiful blue skies, we jumped off the truck and were greeted by a French officer and with wide open arms and a great big smile, he said to us 'Bienvenue Anglais, bienvenue à la Somme.'"

"...I have no idea what you just said Freddie, but it sounded lovely," lushed Marian, romantically.

"Somme?...the Somme river!?," bellowed Ben with a pinch of worry. "I say that's pretty tough going, I met two Irish lads down the cricket club who were on that bloody mud bank, they wouldn't say one word about it until they had half a bottle of gin in their belly...they said it was like walking into hell, bad place to be that...well if I bump into them again I'll mention your name, you never know it could spark a reunion and then I can go around telling everyone what a small world it is."

Slapping a pantomime thigh, Ben smiles trying to lighten the mood. Apathetic, the Greek replies politely.

"That's very kind of you Ben....met them though, I doubt we would have."

"Well it's a lot of ground, a slim chance, but you never know, what regiment were you with?..."

"...I'm no stranger to regiments, but for that particular location the correct deck would be Battalion, 1st Battalion to be specific."

The Horse twitches wide eyed, blinking with disbelief.

"The 1st Battalion? That was the big bad Bill Browns, the Grenadiers!"

Freddie displays a mild smile.

"...It makes me very happy Ben that you know that. Grenadier Guard Light Infantry, served 1915 to 1916, we started the Battle of Ginchy, north of the Somme river, very different to what we were used to, mainly because we had all the new toys with us, those dangerous tank things, they kept spilling oil all over the place and exploding their engines, more harm than good..."

Still in amazement, Ben picks at the specifics with definite gestures.

"Wait one knobbing minute, are you telling me I'm sitting here with a Grenadier of the first wave, blimey Freddo! You might have told us you're a bloody war hero."

The Stallions statement flares a variety of colourful moods; gleeful girlys beam with intrigue, wiggling their chair bottoms in fascination, a reclining Lidman forlornly rubbing his aching blue bulbs at the pin pained prick of hangman trivia and all the while a fussing Ferret shaking a carmine bonce with disagreeable derision.

"No, no I'm sorry but I'm afraid I don't believe this, it sounded very truthful what you just said but I'm detecting a lie."

Glaring at Ferret, the Boss panics out of a low stupor with a forced guffaw in Freddie's direction, hoping desperately for good humour as Larry continues to fuss the font of his own tombstone.

"My guess is you were just a good hard working Private doing his bit weren't you, you don't have to try'n impress us."

"Shut up Larry!" growled Lidman, joined by a flapping Margo.

"Yes, how rude!"

"Freddo, lying, bollocks! I know a purebred when I see one and that man there is no Private!" neighed Ben, hoofing at Freddie as a well vilified

Larry, sinks down apologetically, sipping his apple juice.

Tired of the bleak banter, Marian hangs over the back of Father's chair, moaning with slurred intoxication.

"Can we ple-e-ase change the subject to something happier, something fun and nice and not to do with the you know what, I want to think about nice things, pink things."

"More jazz!" said the bounding Mouse, resting the fate of entertainment once again on the dizzy gramophone.

"Is this where you keep the other records?"

Angelically, she paw pats the high corner of a wide wooden box on top of the drink's cabinet, receiving quick disparagement from a thrown back Cat.

"No Ethel! there's no records in there, the one in the Machine, it's all we have."

"Well I'm not surprised!, damn expensive everywhere," said Ben. "We only have three for ours, it's perverted what the shops have'em up for, I said to the keeper I could hire a full brass band to stand in the corner for 'that' price!"

"Snurrrr..aaurrrr" agreed the Whale.

"...I know you'll think me nosy, but what's in this box then?" Ethel asked, glancing up at its rusted clasp; a middle green Marian growing anxious.

"Nothing I want shown on my Birthday, now please forget it."

"I must admit I'm feeling a tad curious myself, that box up there is far too wide to be a decorative clock and far too tall to be a cutlery set, I wonder what it could be," simmered the Horse with a mischievous wink; Ethel pleading on with little soft stomps.

"Please, pretty please, can we see what it is?"

Flinting his folly eyes, an idea mixed with a crazed half hope expands Daniel's brain box, causing the swift correction of his deflated home stone slouch back to a dominant boss shape.

"Sweetheart...lets show them."

Pulling out a small side table from between two chairs, he creates a productive desk in front of him, grunting impatiently.

"Well!, bring it over then"

Under protest, the unhappy Cat watches on as Ethel, Ben and Buzz, lift, carry and wake up the dusty dark weight of the wooden box, placing it desk way for old man D with a blunt cumbersome thud.

"Right, just a warning, this is very, very old... it's gunna smell."

Achingly stiff the industrial sized clasp loudly snaps back with a crack of black wood. Yawning its grimy hinges, Mr. Box leisurely opens to a standing zoo room of snooperage, a dry scabby odor rising from its core along with confusion as to what on earth 'Mr.' actually is.

Unable to see and needing to know, Freddie stands in kind, stealing nonchalant to view the mysterious innards, his olive nose noting a strong whiff of flaking rust and the sickly custard scent of ancient palm sweat. Panning into his sunshine eyes over Ethel's dolly shoulder, two protruding brass paddles connected by tattered wires to a cast iron frame of screwed down and hellishly penetrated spring coils.

Beginning assembly, DL fishes out a seven inch crank handle with a hexagon shaped insertion, fitting its prominent prick into the boxes equally hexagon side hole followed by two pincered wire ends clamping their crocodile crowns to twin toggles deep down in the machines middle.

"It really does reek something awful, is it a mechanical weaver? Do you feed yarn into it?" said Margo, pinching her beak.

Sharply, Marian corrects with an air of frustration.

"It's an Induction coil, produces electricity when you crank the handle, now put it back..."

Rubbing his chin hoof, Ben beams with delight.

"I say what a great idea! Is it for hooking up the radio if the power goes out? News might be right, we may need this tonight, 'Storm of potential darkness' top headline, I could come up with far better than that, 'Foreign storm may take your light!' There you are Chaps, just off the top of my head you know."

Monitoring a Monsters message at the side of his eye, Lidman runs an apish finger along the hopeful cold crank handle, reaching its tip with a metal caress.

"This machine's a lot older than Radio lad..."

Standing flummoxed, the Stallion shakes a tailored mane.

"Well doch'it all? hooked up to what then?"

"...Hooked up to people" said Marian, somberly.

"How funny, just then, I could have sworn you said 'people'," grinned Margo, nervously.

Coughing the airborne dust particles, Ethel crouches down to read out loud, the peeling lid stained instruction label, creating a terrible chill with every out dated word.

"Property of Spero Medical institute, registered product 1849, Faradic treatment Induction coil for severe abnormalities of the bowels, nervousness (hysteria), non compos mentis behaviour (female use only), oh this is horrible... recommended tongue clamps for three twenty minute sessions of repetitive turning with one minute intervals...I'm not reading anymore of this," Said Ethel, standing up in a mood.

Revolving to Host, a buff tugging red Rat tweaks a single orange eyebrow.

"This Machine does not sound good, why do you have it Cap?"

Cap grumbles with inner aches.

"...It was my Grandmothers, or rather It was 'for' my Grandmother, the details of why she needed it are bit sad and private...when she reached her eighties, messy as things often are, her husband, my Grandfather, John, knew a Dr. Cordwell, who gave this to him in exchange for free accounting, so a device that should really be gathering dust in a museum somewhere has since become something of a family heirloom..."

"Crikey! How does it work?" said Ben, more excited than ever.

"Well Lad, put simply" proceeded Lidman, clear coughing a wet dusty gullet. "The patient would be tied to the bed, their mouth wedged open, their hands strapped to the twin brass paddles, and then the crank. The faster the handle, the higher the 'healing', just another word for pain..."

Blinking softly, Marian smiles in mild memory.

"Father tried it once, we were testing it, to see if it still worked, I was in charge of turning the handle, that was a birthday also, my fifth."

"Hurt?" asked Larry, plainly.

"Course it bloody hurts!," barked Daniel, the relaxed and jovial nature of the room beginning to torment his reserve. "Impossible also, to hold the paddles when the juice starts flowing, that's why they were strapped..."

"Now that sounds like a challenge!," said bronco Ben, committing to four star jumps in the centre of the room, accompanied by a few boxing jabs and a brief leg stretch against the fireplace.

"I bet you anything I can hold on the longest!"

"Don't be stupid! Didn't you hear it's painful," squeaked Buzz with an added flap to a Horsey holla.

"Fuss not Darling, I have a high pain threshold, it's wonderful, best threshold I own, now how much do you weigh Mr. Lidman...I'm guessing fourteen, fifteen stone, big man, good grip, strong willed, how long'ya'tango with them metal devils?"

Daniel's dry dots, dart down to the dreadful device.

"...Well It wouldn't have been long Lad, two, three seconds at the most."

"Well that shouldn't be too hard to beat," said Ben. "I can already smell victory over the boxes pong, now place your bets chaps! How long?"

"I think you'll last six seconds!" eeked Ethel, exuberantly; a kitty cat M, flagging the polar opposite.

"I'm with Margo, I don't see the point of this..."

Ever persistent, Ben presents his pearly row, arms akimbo and full of pep.

"Ladies! It's just a little shock that's all, a fun test of one's own strength against the elements, now hand me those paddles Mr. Lidman, four seconds to beat..."

Proclaiming the brass twins from a near seated Boss, the haggard connecting wires are pulled to their full extent, the bucking Bronco gripping them tight in a wide dramatic, centre room stand.

Abandoning subtly, Daniel sharp eyes the Greek head on, expecting a quiet restlessness or at least covering a long impatience but neither is apparent, as this game within a game unfolds, it is subtle but noticeably entertained, painted calm and cruel with the darkest of colours.

"Come on Mr. Lidman! What are you waiting for" whined the willing patient, apprehensive and wincey.

Ever so gently the furry fist of old man D turns the greasy crank handle, upon the first few turns, the induction emits a loud and familiar click-clack-click, cultivating tension around the room with each rotation of its seven inch L-shape. Still waiting amongst a constant churn of endless clicking, Ben's extroverted manner gets the better of him with an unbridled hair flick of wild chestnut.

"I can't feel anything Chaps, I think it might be br-a-a-a-a!!!"

Two piercing bolts sprint up the Stallion's grip to sing of Zeus in his equestrian brain, youngish peeps and a heavy jaw slamming shut momentarily as the pain inducing brass paddles fall to the ruby floor with a ting tang ting.

"C-c-christ that hurt!"

"Language!" grumped the Ferret, disapprovingly.

"...I have to admit Ben that was no time at all," said an astonished Cat to a hurried Horse seizing the fallen Paddles and resuming a powerful stride.

"I was just taken by surprise that's all, it's ten for Benjo, do it again, I'm ready!"

The insidious clicking begins anew inside the wide wooden box, gradually Ben starts to receive the punishing current, wrist veins swimming with molten pins, his horsey chomp, a growing fountain of alternating agony utterly unbearable to a loving Buzz.

"That's enough Ben, stop!"

"I'm fine!, fine, It just hurts, start counting, someone should be counting!"

"Keep going, I'll start at six...seven...eight..." counted Ethel from the comfort of her chair.

Queasy yellow with a crescendoing cry, the possessed paddles burst from Ben's painful keepage, his proud posing star shape deflating to a seated flop bottom next to a haggish Wifey.

"You are stupid sometimes...you ok?"

Breathy, the Horse continues to unwillingly twitch.

"That was awful! Went on for hours, how long Ethel?"

"Eight seconds, well...eight and a bit."

"Well It ain't the golden ten Chaps but still a tough act to beat, now who's next..."

"I'll have a go!" cried Ethel, casually jumping up to a lashing Marian.

"No Ethel! You're 'not' doing it."

"Someone's got to represent the girls, it might as well be me," replied the Mouse, stubbornly.

Showing a brattish pink tongue to a blinking Ben, she stomps to the middle carpet, taking possession of the cold smelly batons and holding them upside down like oversized pencils as Lidman grinds his grey teeth with a timorous grunt.

"...Are you sure about this girl?"

Ethel moodily stamps the red ruby.

"Yes I'm sure, now chop-chop."

The hunched Father twists a thick hairy neck to a standing daughter, receiving a reluctant shrug to carry on the unnecessary torture.

As the menacing knob dips out of view, behind Lidman's furry knuckles, Ethel's tiny hands start to loosen their writing pinch, little peeps darting from person to person, heart rate quickening as the first click sounds, she panics.

"Stop! Stop! I don't want to do it, sorry... sorry."

Embarrassed and angry with herself, she places the paddles back down on the red rough and quietly sulks back to her velvet chair, a chest patting Marian sighing with relief.

"Oh I'm glad, you don't need to do it Ethel, it's just a painful shock, what's the point..."

"I was worried there for a second, thought you were going to beat my silver eight," chuckled the Horse.

"Now who's up next, how about the birthday boy?..."

Heavy and wide, the Gorilla danes and abstains with a shaking top shell.

"No Lad, once was enough for me...and I wouldn't ask Larry neither."

"Oh come on chappos!, rise to the occasion, where's that fighting spirit!"

Whether fueled by the word 'fighting' or even a near spirit, Ethel stands up again, storming angrily back to the cold tat brass, picking them up in a white knuckled tightness.

"I've got to do it, or I won't be able to sleep tonight, I don't need to last eight seconds, I just need to feel it, and then I've done it...well come on do it! Do it now for Christ sake!"

"Language!" bellowed L.

Dolly grey's burn to buff.

"Shut the hell up!, you greasy old boot! Go on, do it! Turn the bloody handle!!!"

Shutting her pale ash eyes to hide Lidman's turning motion, the dreaded cycle of pain rides round again and again, click...click...click-click-click, SHOCK!

Searing every inch of her petite lab body, the current happily flows from tiny limb to limb, her child sized mouth flaring a heart breaking squeal that makes the Boss stop immediately. Half recovered, Ben stands and takes the smelly paddles as she limps back to her cotted comfort.

"Ouch, ok that hurt, that really hurt, right ok I've done it, I don't care about the time, I can sleep now, sorry about that everyone, sorry Larry, didn't mean that thing I said."

Falling to a cosy chair cushion, she weakly smiles over at Freddie, who sails back an equal sized simmer and raises her a nod of respect.

"Bravo Ethel, you would have made a good Staffy. Are there any other lady's willing," said Ben, waving the stinky paddles around. Frantically the two M's refuse the bucking Bronco.

"Well guess who that leaves, the only one drinking who isn't remotely spiffed, Mr. can-you-play-the-piano-yes-I-can-indeed, Freddo!"

Steepling a black brow, the quiet Greek reviews the dominant handle handed position, held by a sweaty Host.

"Maybe stop, and put it away," objected Lidman, very unconvincingly.

"You can't just let me win!," retorted the Horse. "Come on Freddie, the big 10! Bit of a warning though, these metal doohickeys make your hands smell tangy."

With nil vacillation Fred elevates, stepping to receive the sadist twins. Arms by his side and cool in temperament, he faces a timid pray, judging the ambivalent twitch of his jittery mitt resting on the crank handle.

"Ready-ready Mr. Lidman." Said the Monster.

Click...Click...Click, counting in chorus...One... Two...Three.

The voltage viper strikes again, ravaging the Greek's tall frame with a caning burst of bodily pain, manifesting itself outward in a very different display to the previous patients, his square jaw remains unaffected, his lids never close, only a breathy shiver rapped in resilience and all the while maintaining his golden gaze to an unsettled pray, tormenting him with the smallest of mocking dimples,...Four..Five..Six, adding hate to an air raid churn, the clicks grow closer together until a Grecian spine seizes up, his hands and knees shaking violently, still holding tight as ever with unwavering friendly contours... Eight... Nine...Ten.

"There it is Chaps! My grand victory stolen!"

Eleven...Twelve...Thirteen...Fourteen, sinking into a dangerous trance, unaware of the wide eyed worry blooming around him, Daniel repeats his rampant rotation, round and round the handle goes, the insect clicks becoming one repetitive noise, Fred's red amber filling with full fat agony, his big mouth quivering open as a thin watery stream of blood leaves his left nostril running down a stubbly philtrum.

Marian moves throne way.

"Father It's time to stop...he's won!...Dad stop!"

Untranced by a daughterly touch, Lidman slows the old induction to a full stop, its meandering tattered wires leading to a convulsing Monster struggling to maintain his one murder mentality, a hellish and fastly approaching consequence surprisingly redirected by a loudly clapping and flamboyantly whooping Horse.

"Astonishing! Incredible even, beaten by the best, there's no shame in it!"

"...Ben I think you should open the champagne now, everyone is so, so dry, in fact I'll do it," said Margo, grabbing the green bottle and flee flapping into the kitchen to demurely escape the catalogue of smells and the increasing claustrophobia of the bunting bliss.

"Yes the froggy juice! How did we forget, Marian I'm raiding your cupboards for flute glasses," smiled Ben galloping likewise, followed pussily by an outraged M.

"You're not raiding anything, I'll get them," she said, equally grateful to embrace a new fresh aired setting.

Quietly, a grim wilting Greek carefully shuffles like a chain gang man to sit the edge of his moderate chair, still holding the metallic brown paddles.

"...There's been a lot of bleeding at this party... don't much care for it," Larry remarked, finally finishing his prolonged soft drink.

"I think I'll go and fill this up at the tap, it will be nice to go into the kitchen actually, that

coil thing really smells and I'm about eighty percent sure your next door neighbour's healthy gut
has just added to it, so I'm going in the kitchen."

Grumping up, the treading Ferret creeps
through the threshold.

"...Ethel, could I trouble you for a moment.
The conductors, my hands seem to have become
rather fond of them," Fred said softly, approached
by a chair leaving E.

"Maybe this game wasn't the best idea," said
she in a low privacy.

Greek replies in a similar whisper.

"A game indeed, a wonderful one, it reveals
who people really are inside..."

Prising apart tanned hands the brass twins
are carried back to their wooden wide nest, a weary
DL proceeding to shut, lock and lift to an origi-
nal position, granting the travelling view of Mon-
sterly palms, panting veins like tree limbs along
swollen fingers.

"Your nose...I'll get something," said the Mouse,
scurrying to join the laughing scullery, leaving

Captain and Greek sitting opposite each other in a very rare moment of isolation.

Watching the glowing dead embers in the fireplace grate, Fred wipes the cherry stream with the aid of a white shirt sleeve.

"...Are you enjoying your birthday Mr. Lidman?"

Grey Gorilla turns a shade greyer.

"...Yes...thank you."

Freddie tuts five times, licking his brown lips, correcting a woeful wilt.

"You lie, you don't look like your enjoying yourself."

".... How can I?...how could anyone?" grouched Daniel, miserably.

"Well If my timely present is proving difficult, we could excuse ourselves...take a walk, would you like that Mr. Lidman?"

Trying everything possible to keep from tearing up, the old man shakes his head, retorting in a fine fatigue.

"...Tell me who hired you, I have a right to know..."

Fred leans forward.

"...Be honest with yourself Mr. Lidman, would it make any difference if I told you..."

Sharply Inhaling through wobbling jowls, the old man lowers a pork pie chin ponderously onto his hairy chest. As the rain forest vapour leaves his lulling lungs a moment of clarity gives birth to the next malformed attempt at survival. Raising to rest his thinning crown on the back of a padded throne, he starts to titter and chuckle at the block black severity.

"Do you know what I've just realised...I think this may infact be the very definition of a bad day, me and those words 'It's a bad day', I've strung them together my who-o-ole life, a bad day here and a bad day there, but they're never really, truly bad…I feel exhausted, yes exhausted and oh what's the word…helpless, that's it. It's no interest to you I'm sure, but the last time I truly felt 'helpless' was when my dear wife was giving birth, it's completely out of your hands and there is nothing you can do, especially when ya'old...an old man like me, haven't got long in me anyway, a couple of years at the most, three or four birthdays maybe, but you, you're basically young...a young pup with a nice big dollop of time to change things for the better, I don't think a strong, honest man like you should fuss over a finished old fart like me...an oldy, do you know what you should be doing, let me tell you my Lad, find a good steady girl, full madly in love, raise a few children and live in a beautiful place that you can call 'home', your very own castle my Lad, that's the place to be, not here, I've done it Freddie, I've lived it, and I'm here to tell you now...it's all worth it."

The Greek relaxes back.

"...All great things to have, and what makes you think I haven't?"

Retreating a failed method, Lidman's mental theatre briefly entertains an unfathomable reality were his Monster could have ever been an attentive husband let alone a loving father and subsequently changes tact to a logical judgement.

"...it's inconceivable, a man of your stature committing to the gutter wealth, a poor man's trade, I mean really Fred, you're a Grenadier Guard, did you see the way Ben looked at you, you're a hero, you have to admit, that this...this right here, is no way to carry on with life."

Impatiently, Fred looks at his watch.

"Although I'm thoroughly enjoying these little rants of yours Mr. Lidman, I have to confess I find myself rather confused, why oh why are you talking to me, when you should be spending this very precious time with the people you love..."

Crumbling, Lidman's unhappy heart sinks back down to a drawing board beginning, the only thing up, a standing Greek.

"Now, if you will excuse me, I would like to use your restroom, upstairs at a guess?..."

"...Pardon?" responded Boss, taken aback by the domestic question.

"I said...I'd like to use your restroom, you don't have a problem with me using it do you?..."

"You...you want to use my toilet?...it's upstairs, up the stairs and down the corridor, last door on the right..."

"Thank you," added Greek, moving to the solitary staircase. "I suppose before I let you out of my sight, I should reinforce the colourful ramifications of what would invariably happen if you tried to run or revealed on mass the truth to your beloved guests."

Softly snarling, the Boss's hot rock suffers the imponderable nature of things.

"I do think, but wasn't thinking that..."

"I know you weren't Mr. Lidman, because you are a smart man, very smart, but for argument's sake, let us pretend you really were that foolish, If I returned from your presumably quaint facilities and you weren't here...I would suddenly feel exceedingly tired around the others, it's a strange thing tiredness, it affects people in so many ways, some people talk a little faster, some people have bouts of depression, but me, when I fall tired Mr. Lidman, I suddenly feel an overwhelming urge to splurge, with everything I have about my person, whether it be money, opinions, bullets, I just let my hair down and think to myself, what the hell, I can always buy more and start rattling through them like second chances..."

Ascending stair for stair, Daniel watches the Monster slowly disappear past the top banister, leaving only the sound of creaking along the up stairs landing, fading away out of ear shot.

Horribly alone in every way possible, casting a low silhouette in a dark downy brown arm chair, his fatherly ape shells listen to a far Daughter's lemon drop laughter intermingled with chatter and chimes. Recalling the last time he was completely solo, the strangled pang of past piano playing lights up his prefrontal cortex with a blissful ignorance that no longer exists.

"This is happening...this is actually happening, what can I do, come on Daniel think, what can I do...what can I do?"

To the rhythm of a snoring Betridge, Daniel begins to use a great gaggle of grey matter, a colossal amount of calculated empathy in an effort to understand his lucid executioner, his growing, red hot brain submerging itself in coolant as it tackles a never ending tax return of messy details, such as his Monsters name, his method of manipulation, his nose, clothes and the texture of his skin, everything, but no matter how hard Lidman tried, he couldn't help but feel he was overlooking something, something important, an uncharted island on the mind map of a mad man. Freddie is clearly intelligent he thought, a psychopath, a perfectionist, almost certainly mentally ill, but none the less intelligent, very intelligent, which was precisely the point.

Unpleasantly, Daniel thinks of all the ingenious ways someone could have murdered him before he ever reached the cottage at the end of his work day. Fred could have hired a heavy van and crashed into the old ford round a tight country lane and made it look like an accident, 'he came out of nowhere, I didn't see him' he could have said, he could have put a bomb in his briefcase, rifled him from the rooftops, he could have even marched with a morning yawn into Lidman and Son, pretending to be a tax inspector from the department of something and something, skipped confidently up the grandeur staircase straight into head office and wasted as many bullets as his little black heart desired, no one would've heard over the click-clack-click and then casually strolled out tipping his hat, job done, 'but oh no' he thought, a white cold goblin of a feeling, crawls through Lidman's entire bodily system as he finally stumbles upon the contradicting note, that his Monsters initial intention was in fact to get caught, a desperate attempt at sabotaging his own unstoppable train of heavenless dealings, he has entered into a social tomb, a closed maze, a place of which he has no knowledge of and surrounded himself with interchanging, constantly moving individuals, exchanging observational information every second that he is here, making it impossible for him to carry out the task without lawful consequence and has been trying to achieve the impossible ever since. But the cruelest truth is yet to come and painfully clear to a heavy Host, whatever winding road is taken from this point on, one very vexing outcome stays the same, that he, would in fact, be dead.

CHAPTER SIX:

Up

Resentfully, the upstairs bathroom interior, supports the ferocious foreign entity, from the toilet to the sink, the towel to the soap, they all wish ill will upon their assuredly violent visitor. With held ceramic union, the large tub takes high pride in producing the highest levels of palpable animosity, striving to convert all ambivalent items to its way of thinking, including twelve virtuous violets sitting in a vase, which in themselves are equally foreign, equally organic and equally new, lovingly placed yesterday by a purring Marian. All twelve violets agree that he is indeed horrible, while secretly being relieved that they are no longer the newest element in the room and can now socialise normally without fear of rejection.

The only inanimate inadequacy in regards to completely concurring rests solely with the hexagon floor tiles, which refuse in chorus to renounce the suited soldier of questionable psychosis, as all five hundred and seventy eight of them, respect strength and discipline in whatever form it may take and even show off their own strict, twenty four hour regime by assembling themselves along the lavatory floor in a diligent display of perfect alignment and symmetry.

Meanwhile, the first act of the foreign Fred is to grab the woolly wash towel and strategically cover up the long oval mirror above the sink, his second to stand astride the lifted lid and bowl and following to the inevitable third act of urination.

Letting out a boyish moan of agony, a powerful, steaming, yellow ribbon of painful relief arcs itself up and then down into the ceramic arrangement, the sparkling flow carrying with it an unnatural redness spanning from severely damaged physiology. The racing river quickly turns into a dwindling stream finishing up at a very, very slow, very, very painful, drip-drip-drip as his aching kidney precedes to its regular torment of holding a half load unwilling to relent, leaving him with an excruciating gut and a stinging pin pricked tip.

After a moody, mournful, rebuttoning, Freddie wipes away fresh tears along the blood stained cuff and turns to address the sink with an unhappy soft sniff. In his sad uncomfortableness, he roughly dives an aggravated hand into his inside breast pocket, gratefully glancing up at the freshly hung wash towel before pulling out a black and beaten, Belgian born revolver. Promptly unclipping a hinged cylinder of six empty chambers he flusters once more in the opposite pocket to retrieve a tidy brown leather pouch containing the perfect amount of heavy bronze coloured bullets. Disturbed from their bedded bundle, each one has their life ending virginity taken by an unwashed hand, slotting them slowly into their individual tunnels, click goes the reclipped cylinder.

Taking a small cake slice of time, F sluggishly conceals the black firearm back inside a sweaty blazer, opens the door and exits the bathroom to the soundless sound of saluting hexagons.

Lined with light floral wallpaper, the sweet potpourri scented landing stretches its capacity of twenty seven feet to the sloping staircase down to the Living Room, the homely sight of a few dim doors and five thick picture frames was to be expected, with the unforetold addition of a small petite girl waiting for him at the end of the way, standing side long in a strange profile.

"Ethel I see...everything alright?" said Fred, moving his draconian shoulders closer and closer to her short and frozen wall gaze.

Acknowledging not, Ethel remains unaltered, turned and transfixed, her horizontal obsession given to one of the picture frames. Now close enough to touch, Freddie joins her zombified examination expecting a remarkable sight, instead, a crudely kept copy of 'Whistler's Mother', depicting in oiled strokes an elderly American woman, from a long forgotten time of toil and tears, sitting alone in a rickety ridden rocking chair, her surroundings gloomy, godless and starved of colour.

Blinking rapidly, Ethel squeaks at the sudden side of close proximity.

"Oh it's you! You scared me," she slurred, tipsily.

"I have a tea cloth for your nose...already taken care of it? That's good, Marian would probably kill me, her pretty kitchen cloths, but it was all I could find..."

"Unforgivable, stained at the corners, she would bubble up with rage and throw us both out into the cold," Freddie remarked, making the Mouse smile.

"She wouldn't go that far, no-no..."

Shaking her bonce, the red ruby headscarf slips down over her pale grey eyes.

"Why did I wear this stupid thing?...

Huffing hot, she tries to tighten the back bind.

"I'll do it, turn around," said a pleasant Fred in a failing parental tone.

After a one second meeting between pale grey and sun, she turns her tiny childlike shoulders, the blood stained cuff scuffing the back of her hair bun as he clumsily secures the scarf bindings to a satisfactory tightness. Upon revolving, she quickly rises up on two tippy toes, leans in and kisses the rough sand paper skin of his cheek with a cupid's bow of milk and honey.

"Why?" said the Monster, under his breath.

Ethel smiles angelically.

"For fixing my engine of course."

Monster mirrors the action.

"No 'why' were you looking at this picture?"

"Oh that!...I was just considering something... now come on, you're looking at a girl who was promised a glass of champagne and is still horribly waiting, how I hate waiting," she said, bratishly.

Escorting each other down the solitary staircase, little E holds her breath as if about to be held under water, the drunk low Living Room assaulting at least two if not three of their senses. In an attempt to battle against boredom, she jumps the last few steps, carpet landing into Larry's fatal phrase 'You young people don't know when times were good'.

"Of course we know! For us it's now because we're young and for you it's then because you're old and so on and so on," said Ben, philosophically leaning with the ginger Ferret against a dead fireside.

Satisfied with the sixteen stone mound of farm flubber sufficiently unconscious along a navy Chaise Lounge, the Greek's observation lightly crooks a cosy chair pear, Cat and Buzz sharing the last of the winking tarts. With a kingdom count finishing short a monstrous manner stirs with quick severity only to be soothed back by a shepherding threshold, framing the last wandering sheep preparing a far mystery at the dark windowed sink.

As the one and only jazz record, blares once again from the horny horn flower, Freddie proclaims the most advantageous chair next to Margo in perfect viewing alignment of his pray, a playful Ethel perching her little round bottom on the padded chair arm, inspiring any and all to tap their feet, adding a pedal of sound to the roaring rockery of jazzdom.

But there is...what?...Hello Again, HELLO AGAIN! Hello, Hello Bonjour Mes petits Hello,

Hello, infinity hello again my beautifully brave Comrades! 'I don't understand, I don't like this! Who's talking? Please tell me who's talking?'... Calm, stay calm my darling bubble boys and guillotine girls, it's me of course, me! You remember me don't you, from our early beginnings, marching proudly side by side, falling and running with bare, infant chested war paint and wild warmth in our honey chocolate hearts, please say you remember me, after all I remember you, which is why I so want you to understand me. Please don't think me unfaithful and accept my strongest apologies, if I had knees I would bend them, if I had hands I would clasp them, please, please take my sincerest regret for leaving without telling you. I presume your autopilot journey thus far is sufficient? Sweet food, fun activities, a stewardess for every whim and wiggle, it's important to me that you're happy or at least trying to be happy and know wholeheartedly that my attention was turned by business matters and through no fault of our own, but make up I will, I'll even straighten up for you, to show my loyalty and devotion, making me perfect and prim, there is nothing I lack, your disembodied throb is back.

Now children, I'm looking for my old Ape, have you seen him on your travels? There's no need to answer, I already know where he is, I can smell his early onset of delightfully damp decomposition, let us float up, up, up my bobbing pea sized patriots, let us waft our ghostly selves in the direction of the kitchen, oh that's sickening, I don't like this threshold, the frame's too firm, it's yucky, yucky, a-a-a-and we're through, well done class, stupendo, fantastico, onwards we go, high above the twinkling glass particles to nuzzle up close to this pretty primate, snuffling at his trough of painful preparation.

Captain J Simio! I ador-r-r-re you, my rotting condemned monkey man, that smell drives me insane it does, it does, he's magnificent, I wish I could primitively touch his sunburn blisters and bumps and pretty plump skin boils, I would prick his screaming cysts and suck out the momma milk pus of yellow and green and lick the circular flap clean off from the inside...On no, no, no, no this isn't good my darlings, I'm being called away again, impossible to stay, it's business as usual, but my matters of animarum will pass quite fast I'm sure. Be good, mammy will bring you back a present, ta-ta.

"Maria-a-an! Help me with the champagne, corks stuck," cried Daniel in the direction of the living room.

A spifflicated M pussy paws onto the tiles.

"…Why have you called me to do an act of strength and not one of the men who are all just sitting around doing sod all?"

"Because you have magic fingers" grunts Father, passing the bottle.

Beside a countered selection of fresh flute glasses, she reluctantly struggles with the stubborn cork as well as the catering maintenance of being a good hostess.

"Gosh! It really is stuck…your creepy friend is leaving soon by the way, told me to tell you," said a breathy Marian, resorting to stride the bottles base between her hourglass thighs and white knuckle huff to an eventual pulling pop.

"What!? Who, who's leaving?" said DL, wide eyed.

"Your Friend Larry Dad, it's almost eleven, it's probably past his bed time...my hand hurts now."

Internally panicking at the mathematical prospect of people wanting to leave, adding the end of a party and subsequently subtracting his life, Lidman takes the champagne from a swaying Daughter and begins filling the fresh flute glasses with a rattling thick wrist.

"Sweetheart...your friends, will they be wanting to leave too?"

Kitty slinks on the spot.

"In an hour or so I expect, Ben's got to be up early for work tomorrow...apparently."

Vibrating madly, Lidman's hairy hand tremors away from a fluted rim, pouring a splash of French pleasure onto the careless countertop. Bending bow back with red faced frustration, he hurriedly opens a counter drawer to reach for one of the many floral dish towels to dab up the drizzle, accidentally pulling the third instead of the second in a further act of clumsy ineptitude, not containing beautifully laundered mopperys, the old man ogles desperately down at items of rare use and forgotten folly, a fishing lure in the shape of a green frog, a grubby ball of knotted string, a small box of nails, one gardening glove and finally, an ominously coloured, black and yellow tin of Wallingtons rat poison remedy, stating in big bold letters 'No scent, No colour. For 100% vermin eradication'. Crazy eyed, the Captain slams the drawer, craning up in a coughing sweaty glaze as Marian spots the unsightly spill.

"Why are you making a mess? Do you want me to pour it out...dad?...are you alright? Oh please tell me you haven't caught the Betridge bug."

Father frowns, glistening with a sickly sou.

"I'm fine lass! Stop fussing...who am I pouring this for?"

Leaping a lick of red ruby, kitty Cat M addresses the entire bunt.

"Who wants a glass of bubbly then?!"

"Oh me!, me!, me!" said Ethel, waving her school girl limbs.

Assertively, Stallion stands with a pointing duo digit.

"Two over here as well! The real thing, it's hotsy totsy, got through five bottles at Christmas, most of it due to Margo."

"Your Family! There is no more to say about it," squawked Wifey, followed by Larry's boring bumble.

"...I don't drink."

"Yes I know, you've told us," said Cat, impatiently.

"Freddie...glass of Champagne?"

The Greek eyeballs a clear Kitchen view with a slight apprehension, unable to see his planning prey through the doorway.

"...A glass, that's very kind of you Marian...a glass for me then..."

Daughter returns slavish to a jittery mad Dad, hunched in deep contemplation over the kitchen counter.

"Four glasses Dad..."

Without knowing the numbers, a cracked Cap has already poured the entire contents of the bottle into eleven Champagne flutes with one laying lonely wet and shell shocked at the bottom of the ceramic sink, recovering from a vicious rinsing.

"...Larry doesn't want one...well Larry doesn't drink," said the guest obsessed Father.

Daughter baffles back, starting a tit-tat tennis match.

"What? I didn't say anything about Larry..."

"I see, where is he in the room Marian?" droned a strangely behaving Father, never looking up, focusing on the flutes.

"...Who Larry? He and Ben are just talking nonsense by the fireplace, why?"

"Just trying to be a good Host, so they're by the fireplace and what about the others?..."

"Well Margo and Freddie are sat down watching them squabble and Ethel's just slinking around everyone, we may need to ration her intake soon."

"Ethel?...Yes I know Ethel, the one who looks like a child dressed as an Indian, she needs to drink less, that's good, that's very good..."

"What are you talking about? Are you sure you're alright? You keep shaking."

"...And I assume Mrs. Betridge is still asleep?"

"Yes, she's dead to the world..."

Careful not to spill, Daniel hands two bubbling glasses to a drunken Daughter, grunting his instructions.

"These are for Ben and his wife, don't give them to anyone else, it's their bottle, a drop more for them, understand?"

Nodding dozily, she carries them away through the threshold, catching the end of a purposely bad Ben joke and the great groan that precedes it.

"And then the Vet says...well I'm not surprised! That sausage is three weeks old!"

Wincing at the painfully predictable punchline, a champagne snatching Margo turns her modest birdie sips into seagull gulps, finishing half her glass in an instant.

Growing ever suspicious, Freddie surreptitiously watches Marion's slender movements, leaving for the kitchen once again and then returning almost instantaneously with two more flutes, one containing considerably less Champagne than the other.

"Here you are Ethel," she said swanning to a slinky E. "Sorry it's a bit low, last of the bottle."

"A short drink for a short girl!" said Ben, raising his own.

Ignoring the verbal jab, the Mouse takes her half glass and scurries to the piano stool, proclaiming derrière with a palette resting taste test, every official French note, titillating her tiny pink tongue buds.

"...Well the jokes maybe bad, but this is sublime, I like that word, I will use it more often I think, sublime...subli-i-i-ime."

Long and beautiful, Marian wades through the comfy chairs, a vision of graceful green, handing the last bold beverage to a friendly seated Monster.

"Thank you for my drink Marian, so awfully kind."

Perceptively amongst the sound of six panicking pixies, the Greek tries to detect any trace of malicious intent in her family blue jewels, but finds no trace, at this time or any other.

"Well you're very welcome Freddie," smiled the Cat, stealing piano way to stop a potted Mouse from disturbing anymore high keys.

Afraid of licking the bubbly bottom sooner than intended, Margo banishes her golden half glass to a sluttish side table, nuzzling its left corner against the side of her chair which subsequently and simultaneously rubs its unfaithful right corner, on an even bigger chair, the Monsters chair, Freddie's chair.

Observing the casual placement, Fred forlornly looks up at the tiny microscopic sway of the light fixture with an indistinct glimmer of sadness, disappointment, anger and finally nothing at all, his ever changing eye twinkles noticed across the room by an inebriated Ethel.

"Freddie looks upset everyone, who's upset Fred?"

"...Upset?," said the Monster. "Nothing such, I was just thinking about Ben's jokes that's all, I've always loved jokes, especially long jokes, but I can never remember them and I admire people who can. Know any more Ben?"

"Do I know any? I know tons Freddo! And if you like long ones I've got a right ball bouncer!"

Turning bright pink from Hubby's doltish ways, the meek blushing Buzzard covers her biting beak with an embarrassed wedding wing, each Wifey eye twitch carefully noted by the Greek as a bellowing Horse, rattles off a lengthy list of unfunny fables.

"There's the one about the constipated pig and the one about the Irishman having three wishes, although I shouldn't really tell that one, very, very rude and there's ladies present."

"If it's 'rude' rude, no thank you" said Marian, pondering an absent Father still mopping up the mess.

"I've heard it, you are not telling that joke here," sulked Margo.

"Strictly clean it is! I'll have to blow the dust off my old grammar school Bible jokes, god they were awful, this was the best bad one..."

Clearing his throat with a cheeky wink, Ben sniggers at his own telling.

"Who owned! I say who owned the first ever 'canning' factory Chaps!?"

Brimming with rosy discomposure, Margo's drunk blushery elevates to almost breaking point, all the while a slow Freddie sinking his untouched temptation to the harloting side table sandwiched roughly between the two brainless chairs.

"An interesting joke, about cans, I haven't a clue," remarked the Greek, pleasantly turning to a pulsating punchline bird cracking her beak and shedding fine feathers of inlaid anxiety.

"This is going on forever!," slurred the Mouse. "Just tell us already! Who started the first ever canning factory?"

Vacuuming the air for an impressive breath, the standing Steed widens his showman arms for the fatal finish.

"Noah!, because he had a boat full of preserved pairs!!!"

Snap! Margo's clattering claw plunges past the padding to her aiding alcohol, drawing its golden glisten to her thin lips, taking a thirst quenching, stomach filling gulp from her oddly rejuvenated

French champagne. Licking her brown beak, she darts her dipping lids to the wooden whore still supporting a half full flute.

"Oh no...," she said in a fragile chirp. "So sorry Freddie, I've accidentally drunk your dri.."

With fidgeting breath, her sickly sinking eyes blink and blink again, as an unnaturally loud gut rumble, coils her slowly into the chair, dropping the crying flute with a spill, thud and aching female groans grabbing group attention.

"Oh my! I don't feel well...I think...I think I'm going to be si..."

A diluted burst of yellow bile sprays from her moaning burgundy, forming a filtered mist in the rancid living room air.

"Oh god! Mari I'm sor-r-r..hu! hu!"

As Margo heaves and heaves again, deafened by a ring of raised voices, a second vomiting cascade of half digested tarts projectiles from chin to knee with a painful chair lunge, crashing her prim and proper poise onto the carpet, shaking on all fours like a dying street dog, crying beyond embarrassment, covered from head to toe in personal regurgitation as a flock of panicking, newly sober hands rain down on her groaning front fetal position.

Galloping post haste, Ben veils her shivering back with a warm dinner jacket, the Wife's pale skin chameleonish against the crouching green splash of Marian's dress.

"Margo! What's happened!..."

"It's the beef!," said a shrill Larry, pinching a red roman nose. "I told you it looked wormy, we're probably all going to get it now."

"Mr. Lidman!" yelled Stallion, kitchen way. "Run the tap for a glass old chap, Margo's had a bit of a turn, might be the welly!.."

Bouldering slowly around the door frame, a horrified Lidman is inundated with a chaotic landscape of wailing characters, tip toeing around the puke painted patch with a quick limbed Freddie rubbing the Buzzards back as she sobs on the floor, the site of a disgraced Geisha girl, dry gagging under an arched spine.

"M-m-my stomach really hu-urts," gurgled Margo in a weak, heart-rending whimper.

The caring heads of Mari and Ben appear under her armpits, hoisting the Bird to her expensive heels, revealing the full extent of her lengthy pukerage.

"Best see a doctor, I know a fellow, twenty minute drive tops. It's ok darling! We're going to see Dr. Lawrence from the club," said Ben, suppressing his worried sadness with an assertive vigour.

"I'll come too," added Marian.

Inwardly hating himself for poor Margo and the failed outcome of three people leaving instead of just one, DL interjects with meek trepidation.

"The quack can come here can't he? Surely..."

"No doctor will, it's the middle of the night Dad," cried Marian over the whimpering high pains of a trembling Buzz, hanging her winged weight around a sturdy broad Horse.

"True is! All the docs are sleeping, luckily this one owes me a favour..."

"I can look at her, a simple stomach ache maybe," retorted DL, desperately following the six legged spider formation of Marian, Margo and Ben, sports daying their way into the kitchen with one arachnid arm flinging a countered Champagne rag to a newly tiled Mouse.

"What do you expect me to do with this?"

"Ethel please, just clean a bit will you," said a flustered Marian, little E likewise.

"Clean!?"

"Yes, we won't be long or rather I won't be long, I'm guessing the two of you will be going home after?"

"That's a big Y.E.S, the night's over for us," said Ben, unhappily holding up his greeny white Wife.

Screaming its hinges, the heavy oak entrance bangs open, an opportunistic Wild Wind, swooping head long into a whirling typhoon of coats as Ben bundles Margo over the mud stained mat into the cold blowy atmos.

A doorway Cat turns with a nippy shiver.

"Taking the Ford Dad, it's just following Ben, I'll drive careful and I won't be more than an hour, try not to burn the house down."

"Am I leaving, yes I think I am, yes I think I can," said Ethel, inching to a near hat rack, quickly admonished by a bundled Pussy.

"No! You promised to help me clean up after."

"I know but..."

"No buts! You promised me Ethel Rooster, I won't be long, speedy blooms, bye all..."

Turning to leave, a fatherly voice halts her cold aired exit.

"Marian..."

Unknowingly, the Daughter looks upon her condemned parent.

"What?.."

Terribly tense, Lidman senses Freddie taking an ominous step towards him.

"Well?" said Daughter, the Stallion's car beckoning with loud horn honks from the dead of night drive.

"I...I just wanted to say...Happy Birthday sweetheart..."

With that tiny tender sentence, she disappears into the night.

An irate Ethel still in disbelief at being stranded with two elderly bores, a strange mechanic and a passed out bubba, steals to the glow of the hanging light just in time to see Ben's smiling bobbly head pop out of the drivers seat window as the two vehicles navigate the grey gravel drive in ever consuming darkness.

"Forgot to say chaps! Smashing bash, top marks!"

Screeching their spokes, the night cars turn onto the pebble pelted road and speed off with lucky wheels, far, far away from a multiplying pain partition of ever increasing risk.

Tea towel in hand, Ethel furiously stomps back into the smelly bunting to fulfil the resentful role of washer woman, her wish to leave the house of cakes and carted inebriates profoundly shared with a residual Larry, letting out an ample yawn.

"Well Cap, invite was nice, I get grumpy when tired...so home for me."

Hurriedly, Lidman slams the heavy oak exit, turning to face Ferret in a cold hairy sweat.

"What! You can't leave as well."

"Why's this?" said Grump, scrunching a fussy lip to a lippy Lidman.

"Because you...you need to wait, until Mrs. Betridge wakes up."

Larry corrects a specky rim.

"Why on earth would I need to do that? It's Freddie's Mother and your guest, I don't see why I would have to do anything."

"You need to drive her home Larry! You can't expect us to do it, we've all been drinking, you're the only one who can safely get her out of here," explained Host, acknowledging the sad, sub nature of his words.

"It's only up the road, a gentlemanly thing to do Larry..."

Becoming the second person to be held captive by their own generosity, the Ferret turns to a near Fred, wanting an output of appreciation, finding only a composed amusement, laser beamed at Lidman like a small, cruel, amber eyed child gently smiling with lulled lids at the chesty chirp of a grounded baby chaffinch before swiftly dispatching with a size three bootee.

"This, all of this, I don't comprehend it, if she only lives up the road, why do 'I' have to drive her fat backside there in my Car!" shouted Larry, immediately shocked by his own sour sentence.

"Larry!? It's not like you to make fun of other people's appearance, what's come over you?" rebuked Daniel with a low added brow.

"Sorry! Sorry. I told you I get grumpy and... and rude when I'm tired. Freddie, if I'm going to take your Mother anywhere it's going to be now, I'm ready to leave 'now', so she will have to wake up 'now'."

Managing to combine his own fussy wiggle with an assertive stride, Larry careers into the bunting bliss, almost tripping the heels of a carpet crawling Mouse, gritting her little teeth as she furiously scrubs a mysterious golf ball sized stain off the cream coloured rug.

Ever determined, Larry steals to kneel beside the deep blue Chaise Lounge and gently slaps the Whale's cheek, attempting to jolt her back into consciousness.

"Right, It's time to wake up Mrs!....what's her name again?"

"You may call her Mrs. Betridge," obliged Freddie from under the frame.

"...Wake up Mrs. Berrybridge! I'm going to take you home now, wakey-wakey!" exclaimed Rat in high soprano.

Ethel's mini round face playfully pops up amongst the gang of chairs.

"We're waking her up? This should be interesting..."

Repeatedly the echoing rebound of slap, slap, slap, between two wrinkled surfaces, bounces around the long Chaise Lounge, a buxom farm filly refusing to rouse from her pot-bellied slumber.

"She's not waking up...hang on! Why am I the one doing this? Freddie you should be the one doing this," said Larry, bluntly.

Still heavily hibernating, Betridge throws flabby bear arms around the neck of a leaned in Larry, pulling him in tightly to her large enveloping breasts.

"What is she doing! Get off me at once madam, get off!"

Frightfully unconscious, Mrs. B refuses to relinquish the squirming red Ferret from her gated grasp, birthing a loud sigh in her deep dreamy state followed by an unbridled web of words.

"Oh it's yo-o-ou isn't it my love...I knew you would come back to me," moaned the Whale dancing in the depths of her dream, unaware of her real realm embrace adding a sque-e-e-ze.

"She's too strong!" muffled a boobyed Larry, the big hearted Hippo rocking in REM desperation.

"...Don't leave me...ple-e-ease don't leave me George..."

The bear blue twins of a mortified DL, widen with fear as that very name is uttered through the steepling cries of a grappling Grump.

"My name is not George!...Freddie get your Mother off me at once!!"

Tearing up beneath her prison bar lashes, Betridge wrestles a resistant Larry even closer to her sorrowful sobs.

"You won't le-e-eave me would you Georgey, you wouldn't le-e-eave Mommy would you...like al-l-l the others...please don't leave...Mommy lo-o-oves her little boy...my boy...my only baby boy..."

"Why is she calling you Georgey?" puzzled the Mouse to a doorway Fred, answered hurriedly by a lying Lidman.

"She's half asleep poor Lass! Doesn't know what she's saying, sometimes I..."

Stopped by sudden alarm, Daniel clocks a glaring Greek, suffering a strange headache under the steady frame, his left hand hiding behind a tweeded wire spine, balling up and shaking insanely.

Before Host can soothingly mollify, the tired Monster eerily issues the very, very last of his self control.

"Show Larry your coin collection Mr. Lidman... quickly."

Dying with relief, a creasing Daniel sports confusion as to why Freddie would prolong Larry's stay, concluding a stealthily covered act of kindness, not for himself but for the girl. It would give her time to leave.

"...Yes, the coin room...come along Larry!"

With high pitched exertion the ginger Grump finally pulls free from the sleeping hug of a crying Kraken, fussing up with a head of messy red, instantly denying the petty peruse.

"No, no I've had enough, I'm leaving."

"Larry I vividly remember, you said 'I want to see the collection', obliged I will..."

Bolshie and bold, Lidman steals to grab the Grumps arm while attempting to come across as casual.

"I said no! I'm going home!" yelled the Ferret.

Pulling away, he buff picks passed a threshold Fred to travel tile for tile.

"This is unbelievable!," projected Daniel below banister, not following for fear of further high emotions.

"I actually can't believe it, I re-e-eally can't, I expected more from you Larry, all these years I thought you were a man of devotion, study, an inspiration that I myself admire, but it would appear I was wrong, it would appear that the historical value that is upstairs right now, holds about as much importance to you as a pile of fly covered dog poo!"

Fumbling with a reluctant latch, Chum struggles to ignore the banister barbs as Lidman maintains a passion filled trajectory.

"If you go through that Door you will be a failure! Someone who isn't worthy, someone who doesn't have what it takes to be a true coin collector...you hear me! If you go now it's over for you Larry, I will have no choice but to expel you from the NCA!..."

Newly opened, the front door is angrily slammed by an outraged L, revolving with the reliable surprise of a sex doll.

"I beg your pardon?!"

DL lifts a stubborn snub nose.

"You heard me Corporal! You're weak, and you lack the strength and discipline to call yourself an official member of the National Coin Association!..."

Ethel stifles a chair back snigger as the fuddy duddy Ferret bounds back to Cap in a moody red hue.

"...You can't do that! You wouldn't do that."

"Oh Yes I would, and it wouldn't take much doing either, the Staffordshire branch founder Gareth hates you, finds you tedious, he'd be spanking himself happy if I got shot of ya."

"Gareth hates me?...You can't give me the boot Cap, I know every currency code there is..."

"Then prove it man! Take that sea of knowledge upstairs and start fulfilling what's expected of you."

"Yes Captain," saluted Chum, forlorn and tired.

Simply for the sake of taunting, the Monster presents a one minute grin for the time it takes for the two oldy's to climb the solitary staircase, their O.A.P paws travelling the railing wood, advancing with bended knee clicks onto the lonely landing and beyond, the grey word 'Wonderful' flooding Lidman's overheated steam brain, more time he thought, beautiful golden nuggets of time, another part of the maze to hide, survive and think, think, think.

Chapter Seven:

Ghosts

Fresh from the kitchen tap, a sodden sponge beats down wet upon the loafy leather chair, wiping away vomit spots of ejected confectionery.

"The smell is blaah!," Said the Mouse."...I'm glad most of it went over the cushion, god the stink and I'm hot and I don't want to be doing this, right that's it!..."

Leaping up dizzy, Ethel miserably pulls the feathery flourish from a vermilion headscarf, falling like black propellers passed her pudgy knees, a breathy unwrap revealing on its final lap a cascading mid-length mess of butterscotch curls, completing her dolly shape of Victorian porcelain.

"Arrrh that feel's so-o-o go-o-od, my head can bre-e-eathe," moaned Ethel, vigorously scratching her hatted scalp, meanwhile a jug eared Fred leans against the big bay, listening intently to the ever changing weather.

"Could at least help," E cried, across the sicky bliss.

Turning yellow amber, Freddie grants a lick of attention.

"...Sweet Ethel, the light of the May moon, the envy of all, why oh why are you cleaning up Margo's mess? She's not even your friend."

Sent from a low clean, the grey eyed girly snaps her mini mouse fangs.

"Because Marian is! I don't have many friends... so I try and be there for the ones that do make it that far..."

"Am I not your friend?" said the Monster.

Kicking the Buzzard chair the ossified Doll glares at him with a childlike breathiness.

"No you're not! Don't ask such stupid questions, you're not even an acquaintance..."

Tired, she girlishly throws the damp sponge in F's direction and then herself into a comfy armchair, folding her juvenile limbs in a moody-mood.

"...Nope...no friend of mine," said E, frowning lullaby eyes around a loose lap."...Although for some reason...I do feel annoyingly comfortable around you, almost as if we're similar in some way...maybe we've just met a lot of strange people...bad people."

Mildly intrigued, Fred walks away from the big bay.

"Bad people? A girl like you, I have my doubts."

Tuckered, the chair Mouse slumps to a reclining comfort.

"...Shut up and change the subject...actually give me a cigarette and then change the subject."

Strolling with an upward glance at the shadowy landing, Freddie takes a waiting smoke stick from the mysterious Rolodex, spun two hours ago by a fascinated Stallion.

Proclaimed from a Grecian drop, she drowsily sucks through baby teeth, its papery pearl lit from above by a murderous hand holding a match.

"You look tired, you should go home," said the match man, caring for dim Dolly.

"...If you only knew what was waiting for me, you wouldn't say that, you'd say don't go Ethel, come with me to a faraway land...where the Bananas run free..."

Rolling amber, Freddie takes a reassuring peep at his watch before kneeling down beside her seat, a drunk Ethel reaching to pat his Hellenous curls.

"I like your hair...it's springy..."

"I could you know," said the Greek. "I could take you away somewhere, somewhere exciting, would you like that Ethel?"

Silently nodding, she plays with his lapel.

"Where would you take me?..."

"Where indeed," whispered F, seductively. "A leaf from the book of Marian perhaps, there's a reason why young girls flock to Paris, it's the only place on earth that loves as much as they do..."

"Is that so...exaggerate how wonderful it is, make me smile," droned the sleepy Mouse, taking a puff.

"...Very well, I know exactly where we would stay, a small but tall, privately owned guest house in the centre of Paris no less, built above a bakery, hardly anyone knows it's there, it may as well be lumière des étoiles."

"That sounded pretty...what's special about it?"

"Well it's horribly expensive, luxurious and all you could want, but the 'why' is a thing of simplicity, on the top floor there is a room, a beautiful suite with a lovers balcony, to leave it open in the summer nights is wise, you wake in the morning with a stretch and a yawn, greeted by the heavenly smell of freshly baked bread and a balcony view only found in painted postcards, the whole of Paris, alive, in love, an Eiffeled paradise."

Lethargic, Ethel half blinks at him with the parted lips of a tired child.

"If I wasn't so beat...I'd burst out laughing at what you just said."

"Pray why?" said Fred.

"...It's too sweet in my mouth," said the Mouse.

Freddie holds her lying lolly paw.

"An example then, to ground it in reality, what are you doing tomorrow?"

"...Nothing."

"Then what's stopping you Ethel...hypothetically if we were to bump into each other at Birmingham station tomorrow morning at say eleven, this is hypothetical of course, we could jump on a train to Southampton and then a little boat ride over the sea and before you know it...we'll be in gay Paree enjoying fine cuisine and even finer wine, as you forget all your worldly troubles, like a dot in the distance..."

"You scare me a little..."

"Ethel the words I want to hear are 'My darling Freddie, I can't wait to see your ugly face tomorrow, at eleven sharp, under the arch of platform seven and I better leave now, so I'm not too tired in the morning'..."

In silent fatigue, Ethel stubs the crystal ashtray with what remains of a wilted pleasure, outstretching her beddy bye arms to an attentive wrist grabbing Greek, pulling her up.

Newly vertical she rag doll stumbles with bratish bed groans into the bright kitchen.

"...Margo's mess, the chair," she said, stopping suddenly, Freddie quick to reply to stunt any further dawdling.

"I'll be your choresman, my night is far from over, prediction, me waddling Mrs. Betridge home..."

"Lucky boy-boy...you know Fred most men would be concerned, a young girl night driving...but you're not so you're funny..."

Swaying with forward hiccups, she reaches the cluttered hat rack, slipping on her little beige trench coat and creating a resourceful neck warmer from her Vermillion wrappings.

Wearing the mask of a gentleman, Freddie opens the heavy front door to a warm breezeless night, the air thick with hot humidity. Cocking an olive elbow, little E boozily holds on tight to the Monsters large bicep trying not to fall over as they leave as one onto the grey gravel drive.

What precedes past this point is a distorted image, a matter of manipulation and the roar of ignition, the sweaty sad sight of a small, sleepy drunk girl strapped behind the wheel of a newly unmounted motor.

But why this ridiculum....what? No stop, STOP!... I don't want to go out there...I want to stay here, within the clever structure, you ub I um...I...I can't think northmanni I'm somnium... that's it isn't it, I'm dre-e-eaming, I'm asleep, where I cannot be sure but I'm definitely sleeping, I'm coming to the surface my darlings, I'm coming, I'm coming, I'm coming, I'm here Comrades!!!...I am aware that I'm fart failing as a good host, but my last apology for bouts of absent behaviour was pure and powerful, double it again and you shall be sufficient...why do you look so sad, so glum, you've aged since last we met, how wonderful...sorry...that was rude what I just said wasn't it? See I'm learning, I'm getting better... but to stay t'would be mad, t'would be sickening, I feel restless, I feel unwanted aches, I feel too young to be in the wrinkled grip of an elderly vice, I want to float again my brave boys and girls...upwards through the ceiling I do, up we go, upstairs I am, where is he I wonder with rising thunder, where is my panicking primate, I want to see him, I want to hear his scraping hoofs, clattering to pick up a floppy flaccid key to a welded wonder...how strange it is, I'm having trouble finding the bindings of his swollen purple toes, maybe he's biding and hiding his way from me, how dare he do, I might be slow but I didn't red face you out of my screaming slit, for you to bite at the bit to prove me unfit, Oh hel-l-l-lo landing doors, my oh my what a pretty bathroom...I'm a what!? How rude...he is definitely not in there and he's not in here, for best results I cock my throb, to detect that tiny elusive cough, one door left, the last room Mr. Baboon, gee golly gosh that's a tricky big knob, I best transcend its monkey matter, panic the particles to the other side...Ar-r-r-r-rh there he is class, he may be small and hard to find but there he is nonetheless, standing so proud, so doomed in his thinking room of circles, it's so simple, so elegant...I do believe his balding pet is about to speak, oh how exciting...

"It's not Philip the Great! It's Charles the third... you can tell by the chin," moaned a miserable Larry, wilted over a small cornered school desk, squinting the fine ridges of a Spanish coin under a hot desk lamp.

Surrounded by a semi-circle of sloping coin cases, an equally frustrated Lidman sweats profusely with wound up shirt sleeves, rapping a tippity tap tap, with his logical sole, trying to conjure up a light hearted retort to soothe the boiling pressures of a mentally homebound Larry.

"That market merchants fleeced me again eh! I knew the chin didn't look right, well it's all part of the fun I suppose...my it's hot, why is it so blimmin hot in here?!..."

As a warm Lidman smears broken beads along a gorilla-ish brow, the Grump grows tetchy beneath the burning bulb.

"You, you said that was the last coin..."

"Just one more Larry," said DL, soothing and soothing.

"This is definitely the last one, you're the only man who can decipher its origin, I could show thi.."

"No! I'm leaving!" snapped the red Rat, relinquishing his seated imprisonment to steal across the stuffy coin room to a firmly closed door.

Mortified in a ghostly moment, Daniel bathes in the raping realisation that faithful Chum is the only living thing standing between him and a boarded up coffin.

Pushing his actions to a new found insanity, Host charges up behind the fleeing Ferret, tackling his tired body into the big fat knob, both banging down onto the hard wood floor in a slow motion fumble of old extremities.

"You're not going anywhere! He's going to kill me!," cried Lidman, leaking the secret while clutching two healthy handfuls of buff brown cardigan.

"He's got a gun, listen to me!"

Fidgeting in a beetlish horror, Larry yanks free his pig tailed buff, scrambling to his feet only to be attacked once more into a dusty display case by a hot headed Host, frothing in a wild frenzy.

"Didn't you hear me, a 'god' 'damn' gun!"

"Ou-u-uch! You've bruised my leg...who's got a gun?" spluttered the case bent Ferret.

"Fred-di-i-ie!" whimpered DL in a labored ache of relief, his fate finally out and proud like a dancing nancy.

"Please help me!...I'll give you anything, coins, take the coins, all of them Larry!"

Plunging a raving mitt to a near presentation case, Lidman covers the Ferret's trembling torso with a brimming scoop of silver Japanese yen, each one loudly clattering to the firm floor like metallic rain, causing enough noise to wake even the most catatonic of creatures.

"They're al-l-l yo-o-ours!."

"Help! Somebody help me!" wailed red Ferret, his back cracking under the Gorilla's weight.

Muzzling Grump with a pushing palm, Lidman detects the unmistakable heavy tremor of the front door being aggressively slammed.

"Shhhh be quiet...did you hear that?" whispered Daniel, continuing in a sharp hush.

"Right Larry you need to listen to me very carefully because we haven't got much time, Freddie... wasn't invited to this party, he's a stranger and...I don't know why but he's here to murder me, I've been keeping it quiet all this time because if I told anyone he would start hurting people, you understand don't you Larry, why I kept my mouth shut, it was for you...to keep you safe, ple-e-ease, for old times sake...'help'...'me.'"

Carefully, DL takes his hairy hand away from an orange gob, only to unpause Larry's plea of despair.

"...Help me! He-e-elp!"

"You're not listening to me! He's a mad man, he drugged Mrs. Betridge, he poisoned Marian's Friend and you're next Larry, he's going to kill you!..."

Eerie in movement, the indiscreet sound of footsteps coming up the solitary staircase reaches their telltale ears, growing louder with every ascending thud, the tit tension comparable to a feverish nightmare, winding and winding and winding, together they stare petrified, an unlocked door pooing itself likewise as the maddening metronome of successional thuds, plants its first creak onto the lonely landing.

"...Well lock it then!!!" squealed Larry, believing by way of fear.

Propelling himself, Lidman painfully rams his pensioner thigh between the door and frame, revolving the key and lock to its inevitable click of security. Falling back to the floor, Cap scrambles to the middle of the room as the line of light under the door morphs its strings, struggling to penetrate past a quickening stomp stomp stomp stop. The door handle turns with a tempered bang as the young lock fulfils its quarterly turn before snapping back to a three o'clock tock.

Anxious beyond measure, the L and D duo exchange a haunted empathy only to be jumped again by a second aggravated handle, mixed with a forced shudder of the entire door in its frame.

"...Who is it!?" said Larry with an out of place casualness.

In the ensuing lack of sound, the uneasy coin coop multiplies to a fizzing semen only to be washed away in an instant by an angry pussy.

"What do you mean 'who is it', it's Marian! What's going on? Why was the front door wide open?..."

Regaining himself to a solemn stand, Lidman's paternal heart suffers an ancient pang, wanting to cry the serrated sentence 'Why girl, why did you come back, why didn't you stay away.'

Unbearably suppressing his wishing want, Father ambles to the door, his daddy digits dancing around a brown coloured key.

"Marian! Is...is anyone with you?"

"What?!No there's nobody with me!," shouted the Cat. "Look Dad I've just spent an hour of my life waiting in a doctors conservatory, I'm re-e-eally not in the mood for hide and seek or whatever last minute game this is meant to be, I think everyone needs to go home now, don't you think?!.."

"Where's Freddie sweetheart!?" continued Father, sharply.

"Dad, I'm not going to stand here yelling at you, through a closed door!"

"Just answer me girl! Is Freddie downstairs!?"

"No he's not!..."

Key turned, the door is opened to a night weary Marian, her beautiful oval blues showing a shade of cross to an apprehensive Dadda.

"When you came in, no Fred?" added DL, stepping the landing like an overweight gibbon, browsing an ominous stair view.

"While we are playing this game of where everyone is, where the hell is Ethel? She could have at least stuck around to say goodnight, unbelievable," said Marian, throwing her arms up in a huff.

"And Margo had to have her stomach pumped, I could hear it happening and everything..."

As kitty Cat cringes at the freshly made memory, a banister handed Father inflates a mauve bag of worry.

"But she's alive?"

"...Of course she's alive, Doctor's letting them stay the night though, to keep an eye on her."

Hiding his guilt, Lidman grunts in agreement.

"The cause?..."

"Confidential, a big no-no, the Doctor just kept asking if Margo gets depressed sometimes," replied M suddenly clocking their fearfulness.

"What's wrong?..."

Crazy rose, the red Rat creeps from the coin room.

"He thinks that..."

"Shut up Larry! Don't tell her anything, everyone just be quiet," barked Lidman, planting his first diagonal dip onto the staircase.

"Right, I'm going down...both of you stay here..."

Upset and shrill, Larry cowardly coos from the doorway.

"Don't you worry about that! I'm staying up here, until this is all sorted out!"

Feline eyes dart between cumbersome coo.

"Sorted what out?...Have you two seen a ghost or something?..."

With the big bay displaying rain, wind and the beginning of thunder, Lidman reaches the final creak, swooping living room and kitchen in one panicy peep. Despite the happy fact of an absent Monster, a dry golf ball sized gulp struggles its way down Daniel's sagging gullet, the messy ravagement of the bunting bliss, sufficiently tidy and clean, the cushions pleasantly placed, the troublesome chair thoroughly scrubbed of all buzzardry, even the ashtray is empty, but a thousand times more unnerving then this unsettling odd-ity, is the unmovable mass of Mrs. Betridge 'missing' from the deep blue Chaise Lounge.

"There's no one here?..."

An angry Marian stomps down the staircase.

"Dad I think it's time for bed! You've had way too much to drink.."

"Larry! He's taken Mrs. Betridge!" yelled DL to a high landing Rat.

"He's what?!"

"Someone explain what's going on, now!" fumed Marian, informed by a weaselish woo.

"He thinks Freddie is trying to kill him!..."

"Cork it Larry!!!"

Ever confused, Daughter dimbles.

"Freddie?...Trying to kill you, why? Have you upset him?..."

"Both of you please! Just be quiet, I need to think," growled Lidman, wearily shuffling into the bright kitchen with Larry's moaning drones, lingering on from the top step.

"No Captain! I will not be quiet, you always do this to me, you've always put me in danger, like that old drainage pipe, you ordered me to inspect it for Hun and I got bitten by a badger! I'm sick of it, you hear me!"

Timidly, Daniel approaches the mud stained mat.

"Marian! When you came in....you said the front door was open?"

"Yes! Wide open, it's freezing in here now"

Veering away from the black windowed sink, DL begins to madly mutter, his ape brain holding council, a meeting with its own self.

"...So he's taken Mrs. Betridge outside, why? He's taken her home, but that's, come on think... why would he do that?...To get her out of the way, one less element, but the door has been locked and there's no one here...he...he didn't expect Marian to be back yet...he's been locked out, Marian's locked him out!"

The home bulbs, all of them, illuminating the rods and cones of Lidman's pulsating pupils are in an instant cut short, their glowing tungstens of molten wire die with fading filaments, plunging the Household and all of its occupants, into a terrible blackening.

CHAPTER EIGHT:

Blood and Shadows

The foreign storm with its zig-zag yellow and rumbling curry gut, invites night into every corner of the commodious cottage, duveting its residence beneath a melanoid blanket of black, spearing their clitted ears with the sound of pummeling window rain and the prolonged female soprano of a newly blinded banister hugging red Ferret.

"I can't se-e-e! Oh god I'm bli-i-ind!!!"

"Marian! Are you alright?!" cried Lidman from an obsidian kitchen, trying to force his disabled sight to hone in on a few stray beams of hazy moonlight emanating from the big bay.

"Both of you stop shouting! It's the power out, they said this would happen," replied M, slim and sightless, calculating her current position by aid of an armchair, the weaselly staircase howling back at her.

"Going to happen! Who said?"

Marian floats a disgruntled groan.

"The papers! Front page for the past week, don't you read?..."

The shadow bound stair jabbers and jibbers with up and down whimpers.

"...Only the crosswords, sometimes spot the difference on Sundays, oh I hate the dark! Always have done!..."

Prepared for the black event, the clever Pussy conjures a small hive of tea candles from a pull draw drinks cabinet.

Lighting the first wick willy with a nuzzling burn bobbin, the phosphorus flame illuminates her beautifully worried face from beneath, the grave nothingness surrounding all middle vision made even darker by the sudden output.

Assertive and quick, she places candle after candle around the living room until their budding beams reveal the grim crazy haired spectacle of a gargoyled Ferret, craning half his body down the solitary staircase, maintaining a sweaty grip on the banister's curling top knob.

"Is Freddie down there Captain?!...can you see him?!"

Projecting via kitchen, Daniel's deep reverberation booms from the dark dingle.

"He's outside! Stay away from the windows!..."

"This is ridiculous, wine in berries would Freddie want to kill you?" purred the Cat, only now acknowledging the bunts new found piety, peeled to a black sepia place of Buddhist prayer with bright brush strokes of spooky orange, the shadowy fast candle flickers mimicking the various scare levels in Larry's elderly diction.

"Cap! t..t..tell her what you told me, that 'Freddie' wasn't invited..."

"True our'Lass..." grumbled Father, passing threshold into candlelight, looking older with added illings.

"He's been hired, some carpetbagger wants the building rights to Lidman and Son, year on year I'd never sell, they strung zeros together like pearls, but I was stubborn!"

"Hell I know that look, I hate that look, you're being serious," squirmed the Cat. "I knew there was something odd about him...but I couldn't dart the dot..."

"...The plan was to pop me off in a field," uttered Father, deriving a small fools happiness from the past tense.

Slender aghast, Marian goose bumps in a growing thinkage.

"Well how do you know he's outside? He could still be inside, hiding in the dining room!"

"He wouldn't be," frowned Lidman, eyeing up the coffee dong. "It's a dead end down there, he's too smart, it would give me leverage with advantage, he must be outside..."

Landing Larry, inspects the apocalyptic down pour from a slanted stair view.

"...So...he's just waiting? Out there in the rain."

In resting quietude, three little flames sizzle their wicks and vanish.

"...These tea candles won't last long," said M, placing the last wax waver on the sluttish side table.

Getting faster, Lidman quick wits.

"Gas lamp! The old one in the pantry, might be some paraffin left...if it hasn't dried up."

"I'll go," said Cat, promptly disparaged.

"No! Stay where it's safe girl..."

Nabbing his choice of liberty candle, DL trails once more into the crow black kitchen, keeping a low crouch for fear of being seen by a window winking Monster, presumably vapouring in a hot soaked rage.

Feeling oddly comfortable under the cover of ash black nothingness, Lidman takes to the floor, knuckling a sharp left to the pantry point, grabbing its gray haze handle with an upward reach. Pan door opened, a badly placed sweeper timbers down onto a muscly temple.

"Ou-uch! Bloody broom..."

Inching further with the fumbling form of a blind hunchback, he straightens up warm in the middle willow, fingertips like insect feelers past unwanted tennis rackets and forgotten fishing rods until something smooth, cold, reaches his thumb at the highest point, a long glass tube to his full fancy, making out by tiny candle flame the slightest glint of brass in an otherwise sea of raven shade.

"Got'ya," he whispered.

Sliding the cumbersome lamp from its high shelf amongst a forest of clutter, Lidman's apish mitt fails to obtain the rebellious base.

"Damn it, no, no-o-o."

Toppling, the lamp hurtles like a lead glass phallus, passed the candle and down into pure ebony, wincing in an instant, he waits to hear the vicious connection of heavy brass hitting boarded floor, but nothing, no sound.

Following Mr. Lamp with bended bugger knees, his candle lit perimeter offers no more than a few feet of sight from his own stone grimace. Expecting a cushioning pile of winter coats to alight his parkinson prints, a malleable, meat-like mysterium takes its place along the pantry floor, the ambitious candle, providing enlightenment in the nightmarish form of a Whale, flickering amongst the bric'a'brac with a drip-drip dribble from a dreamy drug smile.

Extinguishing flame with a horrified jolt, DL scrambles bat blind around the noisy nook, trying to find the paraffin lamp. Pan handing in the direction of Betridge, he encounters two objects resting on her large, sleeping, gently breathing belly; protruding rough tongues and the dye scent of leather, Freddie's black leather shoes wafting an unnatural sweetness.

And then potatoes, hundreds of potatoes hitting carpet covered wood, sounding as such to Lidman's hairy shells, the unmistakable bodily repetition of a lingering life falling down the stairs. Panic stricken, he clatters backwards out of the pantry, log flailing to reach the living room.

"Marian! What's happened? Are you..."

Statued by the big bay, Daughter appears paralyzed, her aphroditic holes creasing at the horrid sight of Larry's assaulted body, twisted in a heap on the bottom step, bleeding from a tangled crown.

Stepping red ruby with a weary weight, Father is addressed by a stone faced, bear footed Fred, stood half way up the solitary staircase, pointing the exposed firearm at Marian.

"...That was the last door Mr. Lidman, If I can have you standing together please, there is safety in numbers."

Riddled in peach light and waving swirls of Tibetan red, DL pleads up at the high gallowman.

"Please, oh please. Just let her go, it's me, it's m-e-e-e!"

"...You're trying to be clever again," muttered the Monster.

"The time for calculations has passed Mr. Lidman, stand together please...I won't ask you again."

Joined in misery by a hand hugging Father, Marian bites her gum to the point of bleeding, suitably symbolic of her oozing ambivalence towards aiming amber and subsequent purr in a careful confab.

"...Have...have we upset you Freddie? Angry with us maybe?..."

High Fred beams back at her, confused.

"...I'm not angry Marian, you two have been very hospitable hosts this entire evening."

"...But you...you have that...thing, if this is a Joke," said the Cat, calm as can muster.

"Joke?!," projected Fred, sharply.

"You believe my actions to be a prank Marian, a practical jape...correct?"

Trembling out a small mournful nod, Marian grips her father's sweaty mitt even tighter as Freddie's dark Orange demeanour takes a dramatic turn to a smiling harlequin.

"Well then! Absolutely! It's all just 'one' 'big' 'joke', this isn't even a real gun Marian, it's a toy that I painted black yesterday!" chanted the Monster, laughing and dancing, horribly staged between the ceiling and stair.

Petaled in shape, pink in colour, Marian's mouth laughs along in stark contrast to the rest of her features as Freddie continues to wave his revolvered limb, honking on like an olive skin clown.

"And he fell for it! Can you believe it! Gullible your old Father!..."

Sapph-bulbs old and new, sink momentarily to the bloody Grump and up again to a perplexed F.

"What are you two looking at?... Oh yes, you're right to wonder, why our good friend Larry had to retire for the night, well the reason is clear, that was my first joke, funny, don't you think he looks funny? I do..."

Descending Ethelish, the Greek jumps the last few steps onto the blood red carpet, clearing a vermilion Grump by only a few centimetres, coming closer and closer Lidman fidgets with gritted teeth, Marian ditto with great airy exhales.

"What's wrong with you two? You're not laughing, maybe 'buffooning' is not for me, pity, my dream of touring the music halls will have to be dashed, oh well."

With a careless shrug, Freddie points the Belgian at Father and fires a single round into his shoulder, Bang!!!.

Hitting the floor with an almighty thump of bone and old muscle, Lidman's grey lashes flee from pop eyed pupils, his beautiful brain analysing every foreign iota through a sea of suffering, his pulsating drums mixing the ring of the gunshot with Marian's heartbreaking screams, her soft hands grabbing at his hairy chest and shoulders escalating to a shriek of pain, caused by her own heavenly hair trapped in a dragging fist, pulling her away in a bed of squeals.

"Dad-d-ddy! Daddy Help!, help me!"

A primordial ape rage puppets the Father beyond capability, heaving up and over in a mindless male wail, cricking his vein covered neck to the faded blur of Marian's elegant length wriggling in a rhythmic chair, Fred standing tall, holding the black Belgian to her up and down chest.

"Watch Mr. Lidman, don't miss it..."

"Don't!!!," exclaimed Daniel, creasing in horror.

"A chance like the others, ple-e-ease!..."

Greek turns sallow, coloured in cornish candle light.

"...If you care to cast back, you will remember she has already been given her chance."

"Then I ask again! 'Let' 'her' 'live,' I'll give you anything...anything!"

Surveying the fallen flop, a seeping pray, Fred plays with a pinch of interest.

"...What could you give?...Mr. Lidman, what could you possibly offer, that would make me stop what 'you' started..."

Grasping a grain of hope, Daniel drags his failing build along the blood red carpet, a genuine shade trailing in a long smear.

"I have something! Just let me get it...ple-e-ease just let me get it for you!.."

Reaching the red headed heap like a leaking sandbag, Father submerges his hairy hand under buff brown wool. Curious-curious, Freddie takes the beaten banger away from Marian, aiming at Lidman with a cruel smile, a kid cowboy.

Carefully crawling back, Host unwraps the small square packet, a coughing vision for pity and pine, holding high the green black ravagement to a towering gunman.

"This, this Lad...is one of the ra-a-arest coins in existence, it's called a Silver Samos, 7th century BC, only a few have ever been found, it's worth a fortune Freddie, you could live as kings do my Lad...you could have anything, anything that life can offer."

Disappointed, the Greek vacillates in a breathy boredom.

"...Why do you persist with the old, you should like new things, like me..."

"But it's!.."

"Shh-h-h don't talk...put it in your mouth Mr. Lidman."

"Ah?.."

Freddie rubs the sharp Belgian born along Daniel's thinning hairline.

"Mr. Lidman your hearing isn't that bad, put the coin in your mouth please..."

Down and desperate, D's freckled tongue cots the corrosive coin, the repugnant metallic tang forcing a succession of dry gags, the vile spice of a trillion finger tips.

The Greek channels the drawn out drone of a patronising parent.

"Th-a-ats a good boy, now swallow it down."

Chair bound, the Cat unwillingly watches as Father splutters and heaves on cracking knees to painfully pass the callus coin through a bone dry throat. Managing to lubricate the coarse consumption with resultant vomit, his whole being shivering as the cold currency settles at the bottom of a red aching stomach. All the while a black barrel scraping around on his heavily creased beetle bonce.

A tickled Fred, a slight titter with almond cheek twitches.

"Pathetic with pretty bobbles, you truly are Mr. Lidman...But I have some good news for you, you've managed to stall me long enough to ponder possibilities, a reason for saving your daughter's life."

Clamping a tangled shoulder with a running red mitt, Daniel sighs in a dry relief.

"Oh tha-a-ank you, thank you..."

"...You thank me without knowing. It is important to note that any hope of her surviving this night, is at the mercy of my own personal experiments, and nothing to do with sympathy, sentiment or anything else."

"Anything!" moaned DL with gritted teeth. "You can do 'anything' to her, as long as she lives."

"Dad!!!" screamed Marian, fighting the impulse to get up and run, the gun, the gun, the big bad gun.

"It's going to be ok Sweetie, whatever he wants, don't fight back, just...just let him do It," dribbled the dying Father, paddling in his own drippage.

"Oh no Mr. Lidman...you're the one who is going to be doing it," said the Monster, puzzling a Daddy down-down.

"...Do what?"

"...You'll see...why don't you crawl your clever self over to her, relax, make comfort."

Agonised in candled satsuma, Daniel tows his lulling log body to the arm of her chair. Cockling hands with willy whimpers, both monitor a moving Monster in droopy eyed confusion. Ever calm, Freddie takes a power glad position in the adjacent chair, leaving a spacious gap between him and Host.

"...What you two must be thinking in this moment, the darkest corners of the mind offer strange entertainments...luckily for you and your

Daughter Mr. Lidman, I never acquired a taste for such meaningless spectacles..."

Still pointing the black banger, Freddie presents from his jacket pocket a long white box, big enough to hold a fat fountain pen.

"Since you're so fond of rare things Mr. Lidman, you might take a particular interest in what I'm about to show you...I will spare your child's life because I want to test the effects of something...a drug, a new drug to be specific, only just born, its region, a rather questionable area of eastern China, and one's ownership is painfully transparent, my whole life for one reason or another has involved doing and remembering unspeakable and sometimes hauntingly irreversible things to good people, soft people, just like you two...and alas, it has become necessary for me to induce colourful sedatives in order to sleep at night, the body becomes resistant after a while so I keep having to seek out progressively worse wonders..."

Pearly box opened, a syringe full of clear liquid is taken away from its binding staples.

"This little lily has a wonderful Asian name that I have absolutely no intention of trying to pronounce, but I've just been gifted a very generous amount and assured wholeheartedly that it works in exactly the same way as my previous mixture. Before it stopped working that is, and fortunately for you Marian I haven't tried it yet... it needs to be tested, always wise to gild a guinea pig, which brings me to this very unhappy disclaimer, assuming the manufacturer has done a good job opposed to a very, very, bad job, there is a half percentage the drug will result in complications, an anaphylactic shock if her body tries to reject it, her heart will stop Mr. Lidman...it will simply stop, and that will be that...no more Marian."

Casual as can be, as if serving tea, Freddie frees a far from fine needle of its contraceptive pipe cork, holding it long to a dying Dadda, revolver at the ready.

"Go ahead Mr. Lidman, take it."

Breathing patchy, Marian sobs in silent anguish, the grey glass syringe taken from the Greek's unwashed whittle.

"It is to be administered into the inner forearm, a soft kiwi, now usually a tourniquet would be required but hyperventilation is a helpful alternative, you shouldn't have any problem finding a line."

Showing rows of rich ivory, Marian's youthful body squirms in a ripening unrest, the scarlet Father kneeling up to hold her down with slipping smearing cherry limbs.

"Swe-e-eetheart!," bleated Father in a red faced squalor.

"I...I promise...all will be...all will be..."

Together trembling, Lidman stretches out the slender porcelain, Daughters pink peeps streaming with tired tears, her quivering rose ribbon lips stuttering over every palated tongue tip.

"Da..da..dy, I'm sc..scared.."

A blubbering Father, a runny nose, the same rattling thick wrist.

"...I...I know it, I do, ple-e-ease hold still Sweetheart..."

Physician F, reclining with pleasure.

"Go-o-od Mr. Lidman, keep going, I want to see a steady hand, once you have proclaimed and penetrated the vein at a twenty-five degree angle, I want you to 'very slowly' push the plunger down to its full extent and then smooth as silk out with the needle at precisely the same angle."

Wrenching her arm away, Marian sporadically screams through her lack of breath.

"Help!!! Please somebody help me!!!"

Strangely worried, Fred furiously points the Belgian born at her hot heaving heart.

"I'll shoot!..."

At the height of despair, Daniel claps his hard hand over Marian's mouth, pushing her deep into the chair. Amongst hair, teeth and sweaty palm she bites one of his stubby fingers in the saddest, slightest, least harming way, merely a miserable clamp of father familiarity and love.

"Ple-e-ease Sweet, stop 'please' 'stop', this is the only way," whimpered DL, broken with grief.

Jaw perpetually open as if in a muted scream, she sinks back into the candle lit tragedy, holding out her shaking length to a doctoring Dadda, a clip board chore, squinting and squeezing her faded arm lines.

Riding his chair rim, Freddie watches with the judgemental gaze of a Nursing exam. Miss needle pricks and penetrates, Marian's head hinges back, floating a single ember of pain, slowly the plunger plummets, the clear mysterium disappearing into her puzzled bloodstream, agony, ache and finally out with perfect jerk geometry.

Brightening a weak smile, Freddie beams a caring sincerity.

"...You're both doing splendidly, you have my recognition."

Plastered in dry tears, Marian helplessly concentrates on her inner workings, a chair side parent grabbing her new fizzing fingers, tight grip diluting, strength going down, her ribbage coming up in violent nostril flaring palpitations. Overjoyed, a monstrous midwife directs the suffering in a barrage of hoity hoots.

"Don't go any further Marian! We're going for little breaths...calm it, calm it again...little breaths... little breaths."

"I can't....I cun feely..aym...my armm," droned the Daughter, speech disappearing, glaring petrified at her numb nerve knuckles being brutally stroked, nothing, a rubber limb, empty.

"A good sign," said the happy midwife.

"Her body's accepting it, and now...we can begin."

Hugging his melting girl around the shoulders, Lidman rests a soundless sob on M's warm collarbone. Her heart shaped display begins to show no signs of wain or worry, transforming its style to a nonchalant boredom, glancing around the bunting bliss as if seeing it for the first time.

Professional, the Greek leers in a forward focus.

"Fall away Mr. Lidman, this is the part I'm interested in."

Unwrapping himself from her, Father alarms at the hollowed out horror.

"Sweetheart. Are you?..."

Tenderly turning Marian's chin to him, she simmers with a dispassionate pout, a restaurant Greek clicking his fingers to turn attention.

"...Marian, would you be kind enough to look over here please,"

Languidly, she flops her head to F's eye line.

"...A Question...can you move any part of your lower half?"

Shaking blond locks with a great big grin, she giggles like a mischievous child hiding a secret, beyond broken, Daniel buries his face in his hands.

"Very good Marian, a star for hard work," said Freddie, low-key and calm.

"You should have about ten to twenty seconds left, before you slip away into unconsciousness, I need you to listen carefully to the words I'm about to say, your reaction is very important to me, do you understand?"

She affirms with a bobbing fem neck. Pleased, Freddie continues.

"Listen close then...when you wake up Marian...you won't have a Father anymore...when you wake up you'll be an orphan and all alone in this world...with nobody to hold you...with nobody to love you..."

Marian's golden waves fall back to a low Dadda, the hellenous words having no effect, a bored Daughter, pout blinking, slight and still.

"Look at her Mr. Lidman, isn't it fascinating, she doesn't care...she doesn't feel pain, she doesn't feel fear...she doesn't feel regret...money well spent for those that seek it."

Pale peeps closing into a deep sleep, Lidman repeatedly kisses the back of her flaccid skin fist.

"Goodbye Sweetheart...my darling girl."

Amber eyes sparkle in the red Orange bliss, chair leaned and loose, almost melancholy.

"A-a-a-and off she goes, beautiful, absolutely beautiful...I must confess being impressed, far more feisty by a good five seconds or so...lily-lily."

Quiet again, two more candles wave their last. Black wicks abandoned by wispy smoke strings.

Erratically, the Monster stands, stretching the small of his back, cutting a white scare moan through the newly rested silence before extending a lengthy arm to a grounded DL.

"Could you pass my personal syringe please... I've grown somewhat attached to it..."

Exceedingly feeble, Lidman weakly hands back the soiled shot to a prick picking Greek, standing tall and fit, openly admiring his logical watch.

"12:59 exactly...and that's everybody...yes I do believe that's everybody."

Rough jowl and bristle, Marian's hollow hand suffers one last fatherly kiss. Content with her slumbering safety, a mass of shouldered anguish returns to Lidman's sodden slump with the added vexation of Freddie's mad mutterings.

"But just to be sure, let us summarize for a moment...Mrs. Betridge is quite sufficiently tranquillised, a rather cheeky American blend meant for moose if it's of any interest. Little Ethel is hurtling home drunk in a half clapped out mustard monstrosity. That delightful though slightly irritating young couple Ben and Margo are bound to a doctors bedside, because of what I assume was some sort of garden Insect deterrent?..."

"...Rat poison," growled low Lidman.

A Mediterranean brow, up in amusement.

"Oh rat poison was it, on this flooding day of thunder, how fitting. Your charming child has successfully sampled my untainted batch and finally your cowardly loyal Larry is..."

"Dead!"

"Dead? He's not dead, at least I don't think he is," Said Fred, strolling bear footed to a tangled mound, checking a presumed pulse along a freckled forearm.

"Ye-e-es it's still there, only just though."

Returning throne way, reclining with a pondering austerity, Freddie lays the revolver on the right side of the chair, comfortably taking from his left breasted blazer the last cigar of Daniel J Lidman, given to him seven long hours ago for successfully entering undetected. Lighting his prize by candlelight, he revolves the dark hickory rap between digits of dry urine, a cream smoke ghost escaping via the side of his jailing bite, while enjoying the debilitated pant of a slowly dying Daniel.

Rare hisses served with a pot of pain.

"...I must say Captain, your persistence tonight, has exhausted me, congratulations, a very hard thing to accomplish in such a plain domestic setting, I've even grown to admire how resourceful you are. I wish...I could have you last in my memory as the cleverest creature I ever crushed. But I'm afraid it would be a falsehood, there was...someone, a good few years ago, a Priest, now he was clever...very, very clever, old, about your age...but very fit and taller, much taller, a good six foot something, a deep voice and deep set eyes and a big rosacea nose, hair as white as heaven...his likeness stays with me, to forget such a clever Priest would be a sin...he even managed to give me this..."

Sliding the Havana to one side of his clamping jaws, Freddie unbuttons his shirt, one button, two buttons, three buttons, parting the cotton, a badly healed, brown puncture mark the size of a large marble tarnishes the lower rack of his olive skin ribs.

"Fire poker!," mumbled a cigar mouthed Freddie with a hint of pride.

"He caught me in a moment of remorse. He too was very good at giving long, passionate rants about forgiveness, love and a better life."

"Hope it really hurt," smirked the broken-hearted Father.

"Oh It did, It really did...you were right by the way, this is a very nice cigar, it's got a sort of oaky appley taste to it..."

Anemic with a lack of breath, Lidman speaks a low irritation.

"...Guessing our'Lad..."

"Guessing?" said the Greek, not really paying attention.

"Guessing your lot," Host wallowed. "Army... treated you badly after? All those years of service and then kit bag out, you out, without a penny in your pocket and 'you' being the hardened Guard couldn't earn an honest living..."

Puff kissing a cloud of grey smoke in DL's direction, Fred remains apathetic with the exception of one tapping toe.

"...The army think I'm dead Mr. Lidman, so for all prime and purpose you're being killed by a ghost tonight..."

In helpless stagnation, Liman grows increasingly maddened by the Greeks jovial demeanour, smacking and licking his brown lips, contemplating a slight Raspberry tang to the Havana.

"...Know what I'm starting to think Lad," grumbled the Graveman.

"What's that Captain?.."

"I'm woolgathering...you're not going to kill me at all, I've suddenly clocked that for all your actions you haven't actually killed anyone...and now it's just you, me and that bloody gun!...And all your doing is talking, just talking!, and talking! Why!?"

Regretting every foolish word, the old man cowers, dreading a red reaction.

"...All right Mr. Lidman, since you've asked so passionately, I'll let you in on my private process, my guiding lines, the rules of elimination. We are talking now because I can't stomach the namelessness anymore, the faces, going in and out seeing their one look of terror, it rots one's perspective after a while, you see contrary to what you might think, it becomes progressively easier to dispose of someone once you have dined in the crook of their care. It allows you to collect their flaws, their foibles, their treatment of others, it can all be rolled into one big magnificent ball of justification, after all, we all have imperfections in our character, take our good friend the tall Priest for example, he was a good gallant man in the main, kind and generous, trustworthy, had many fine friends, a well respected saint valued by all, he did however have a rather nasty hidden habit of buttonholing child choirboys scattered through out his past, five different parishes, all presumably silenced by the fear, the fear of being struck down by god almighty, friction burns passed off as playground fumbles. But it was his last vestry adventure a few years ago that relates to 'my' involvement, you see he got a bit overzealous with his fun and fruitful activities and accidentally ended the life of a seven year old, a little girl. Fearing embarrassment, the church of course swept it ruggish and off he skipped to parish number six, his first night there, all nice and comfy, still laying out his books..."

Hiding a despondent mood, Freddie stubs the cigar into the padded chair arm, his dirty brown foot tapping rapid.

"..But despite these frolicsome facts, when I visited his new parochial house at precisely midnight, all he would have got from me is a nice clean bullet, that is...if he hadn't got playful with steely decor...but because he did, I gave him a generous amount of my very, very valuable time, not too much mind you, because as you can imagine I did need to seek quite urgent medical aid, but in the time we spent together I genuinely lost my entire sanity...he was...I...I struggle to find the words I really do...I inflicted so much yellow horror on that man of god, that to this very day Mr. Lidman, to this very day, he isn't actually, technically, dead. Which is very unlike me, not to complete an assigned brief, but the parents...sorry I meant to say employers, as soon as my 'employers' perused his condition from afar, they were big happy faces, warm and satisfied, I even had a hand written letter passed along to me, personally thanking me from the bottom of their little broken hearts..."

Tears, Freddie wipes his lion eyes of golden citrine, somehow made darker by the sparkling swell.

"...I am, evil, Mr. Lidman, there is no getting away from that, that is what I am...I sometimes ponder a day where I will be made to repent by one force or another, and on that day I will, on my knees, I will burn with regret for every stick, stone and broken bone...but not that night...I'm not letting them have that, for that, I am proud."

CHAPTER NINE:

Hold On

Traumatised, the homely wall clock reaches its climactic responsibility, spearing a long downward erection to the ungodly descension of 2am. Worse than ever the weather attacks the window glass, pummeling the living room bay with formidable villains, the ready rain, the wild wind, a marriage of thunder.

Surrounded by shy candle flames, a shadowy den of unconscious creatures, the ante meridiem Fred aggressively smears his tears away, laughing to himself, the faces of past employments dancing around the dying room of his mind, a carpeted Father looking on as the Greek hits himself over the dome with loud cracking slaps, bullying his black brain from turning mutinous, grimacing with a tickling tongue to the left of his mouth with the added wag of a girthy digit.

"There is no need to worry Captain, the environment may be harsh at this time, but I am a reliable service and I will not break up on you... you have my word."

Mentally forlorn, physically flat, Lidman endures the dragged out torture of being killed at any moment, half wanting to scream 'just do it! Just do it!' hearing Freddie's endless workings, the gears are turning thudding down on him and all the while avoiding bulb ties with his Monster for fear of provoking the final fatality. Instead, a fallen gaze to a cascading hem, the emerald dress of his little princess, whispering to her under his breath in the tiniest tones more spirit than sound.

"I'm sorry...my girl, I tried everything...I really did."

"Everything?," Freddie remarked, his jug handle ears picking up every word to DL's disbelief.

"If we're counting maneuvers Mr. Lidman, you're near to everything but not quite, to save what little is left of your life, there remains a singular note, do not mistake me you have done very well, you have tried persuading me, guilting me, threatening me, electrocution, bribery, you even tried poisoning me but what's left Captain... come on...what's the one lever left to pull, the very last thing you could do, to prevent me from filling your face and groin with black red holes for your sweet sleeping beauty, to give her a wonderful surprise for when she wakes up, just like Christmas morning.

Twinging sore, Daniel jostles up to a sweaty sit, his hazy brain box barely obtaining any comprehension.

"I don't know what...what it is..."

"O-o-oh come now, I would have thought it was obvious, well I'll bob a hint, what if I told you I live a very lonely life Mr. Lidman, with very little company."

"...No surprise," D grunted, sourly.

"Yes well, as you can imagine Captain, one gets lonesome, sometimes I cry at night, suck my thumb, hug my teddy bear...what's the word I'm looking for, tense! That's it, I feel tense, so if you were to...some what...loosen up my tension, it may just modify my mood..."

Wincing with dehydration, Daniel's stomach grows sickly, acetic, green in feeling.

"...What on earth are you suggesting..."

"Well it's very straightforward, I'm proposing that you get on all fours to simulate a lesser being, which you are obviously not, and crawl your desperate self across the floor to my pretty parted lap and then...the advised way I would suggest would be to very, very carefully, fish out my privates, and using that clever instrument of linguistic wonder that you have so often played tonight, I want you to relax me...if the experience is suitably pleasurable, it might miraculously put me in not only a good mood Mr. Lidman but also a 'merciful' one as well..."

Glistening, Daniel's dying dial reflects many things, from red eyed exhaustion to liquidised fear, hate and finally a milky white moment of forced contemplation of committing such a perverted act to survive, the mere image racing his rotten heart to the point of flailing spit gnashers.

"You're sick! Disgusting! You're a god damn lizard!!!...You re-e-e-eally enjoy it don't you, you should've died in the War! You shouldn't of liv..."

An Interrupting trig is turned to the hazardous trajectory of DL's chest.

"Well I suppose this is it then," Said Fred, casually. "I think I'll aim for your ticking brain."

Weak from consistent blood loss, the near fainting old man curls forward like a whimpering Muslim at prayer, maintaining a reached grip to the high chair arm, intertwining a tight sedated clasp around Marian's pink paw. The Greek's proceeding verbiage, orderly, prim and sharp to old ears.

"And since you're s-o-o-o fond of your completely deserved captaincy, I will execute you as a military man, just as a firing squad would do for desertion...I even know all the words..."

On the edge of his chair, the Monster cock clicks the black Belgian, pointing at the curved shirted beetle back of old man D.

"Company ready!!!" shouted F, at the height of his lungs, drowning the sound of daughterly digits cracking inside a gorilla-ish grip, the purest of ended fear triggering a loose toilet bowel as Daniel begins to defecate into his sweaty work trousers.

"Aim!!!..."

"...All right!!!...I'll do it!!! I'll do it! Ple-e-ease!" begged Lidman, gasping powerless, every inch of his blood congealed body quivering on the wet Carpet.

"...Do 'what' Mr. Lidman?"

"Th...th...that thing, please...ple-e-ease."

Flaring a Mediterranean whiff, F notes the waft of excretion, its direction traceable, a freshly laid log now newly hammocked in Daniel's underpants.

Quizzical amber.

"Is that yo-o-ou?..."

Blubbing, Daniel breaks down in tears, covering his wrinkled shame.

"It i-s-s isn't it," Freddie declared, sniffing vigorously with revulsion as Lidman bumbles and stutters every tearful gimpage.

"I'm..s..sorry, p..p..please don't kill me, I'll do...it."

"Do it?...I can't think what you're referring to...wait a moment, are you boncing about life saving fellatio Mr. Lidman? You are aren't you, you filthy old brum-brum."

Fighting the urge to pass out, a willing Lidman rocks forward onto his blood dyed knuckles.

"A game Host are we? Well you can give it a go, but I might as well tell you now, your chances of deriving my mercy have significantly decreased now that you smell of stool..."

Freddie leans back, Belgian on guard.

"Well...what are you waiting for Captain..."

Taut, the tension of stretching tweed turning on padded cowhide calls to the Ape's elderly shells as Freddie opens his muscular legs. Wheezing in pain Lidman crawls with a bowed neck, a crude carpet view, one fist, one knee and so on, along the rosary weaves, his quaking wrists struggling to take the weight of his raw torso admitting maypoled ribbons of rich scarlet running passed his elbow, creating the perfect red ruby mark of a bad day trailing behind him.

Almost feminine, Fred whispers in long hisses.

"That's it...that's it...just a little further, there's no need to be scared, look I'll even stop pointing the gun at you, to make you feel a bit more at home."

With every advancing inch print, the Monster's breathe-heave picks up speed, his tanned lips retreating over large teeth as Lidman's wattled woe stops between tweeded knees, rising with running nose water to meet Freddie's morphing demeanour, turning from jupe to jade, a boiling raving rage. Nose diving, the black Belgian swoops head long into a live side of liver spots, sending Host battered across the bliss with a freshly made wound, a biblical fountain stifled by rattling hair rods.

"You were actually going to...to...di-i-isgusting!" screamed the Greek, leaping up bare foot, glaring, spitting, taking long galloping kicks to the middle of his victim, each malleted haymaker, brutal and bronzed by dying candlelight, a hairy DL wheezing winded yelps of sharp pain, his blue body bullied into a deep, dark, corner.

Convulsing onto a flopping front a long object flings from his daily blazer. Swaying forced focus around a glinting guile, a leather sheath, an elephant's head handle of silver, the regifted letter opener now clear as cut crystal in front of him.

Borrowing strength from nil and nothing, an overdrawn Daniel fly fishes a heavy hand to fight the tall cause of his own man made oblivion. Snatching the Elephant with a shedded sheath, he fumbles around with new born bruises, a snarling simian, holding up the blunt blade of shining silver, his left blue jewel horribly darkened by a multitude of burst blood vessels.

"W-e-e-ell, well," said the Greek. "Would you look at that, right at the last...a true soldier."

Despite all effort, a pale Lidman's left arm falls to a paralysed hang. A spent man, frazzled, his gift of breathing botched by a pricking rib.

"I can't...go anymore...just let me hold my girl...when you do it, please...my Sweetheart..."

Tea lights depleting, darker and darker still, a black Daniel crawls a carpeted sea of burning rouge to clutch with his last working limb Marian's slender ankle. Disrupted in hell, a monstrous room shadow, shrieks and kicks his leaking lumber back into the sooted corner in a droplet mist of blood and spit.

"Enough!!!" Freddie crazed, angry and obtusely afraid.

Mono sight fixed to a block black ceiling, Lidman lays motionless. Deprived of a comforting touch, he begins to search all recorded memory for something, anything to play and play again until the inevitable end, his burnt pie of a cerebellum circling a late wife, the filing thought chosen as plain as parcel paper. Not the way she smiled upon first sight, nor their modest wedding day in a small Irish town or even the prolonged birth of mini Marian, where all three were finally complete and together at last. It is by random selection, the short verse song she used to carol quietly to herself to aid the passing of time, the lyrics completely unique to her childhood, invented one sunny summer, a little girl, a scraped knee, a graceful Grandmother wrapping it up with a loving kiss

"Didaly d-o-oo and didaly de-e-ee I do believe I've hurt my kne-e-e, feeling sick and feeling sorrow with Nanna's help I'll see tomorrow," mumbled a dark DL in a warm drooling whisper.

With the end of lyrics scuttling from his blood bubble lips, the old man waits and waits, leisurely dying in a rare brand of silence, only ever conjured by the earliest hours, that weatherless calm, that nothingness. In the murky Bliss of two surviving candles, he hears his Monsters voice again.

"Where is your reference?..."

"...Hu?"

"That rhyme Mr. Lidman...your reference? Where did you hear it?..." Freddie questioned, rapping his long fingernails in the dark, click-clack-click along the sweaty black banger.

"...My...my wife...used to sing it," replied DL in a coarse croak followed by hefty coughing and a loud intake of air.

"...Nanna?...Your wife?...What are the chances, slim as slim can be...was she a nurse? V.A.D, short, stocky, thick Irish accent...ti-i-iny mole on the side of her chin."

Haunting him further, a correct creeper sets off a wailing Lidman, his heavy weight squirming in little writhes, unable to lift any part of himself, frantically blinking, breathing in huge gulps, his weak heart painfully racing in a broken cage.

."...How do you know that?...Did...did you hurt her?!"

"...On the contrary Mr. Lidman, if we are indeed talking about the same woman...she saved my life, and a great many others...now that truly is a fated thing."

"...How dare you...talk...about my wife," bleated a faint Daniel, speech waning away, string by string.

The last two candles, poof-poof.

"...So many nurses, so little clients in comparison," said the darkness. "We're going back a long time now, back to that river, la fin de tout. Ben thought two privates might have known me, met me, shaken my hand, no chance of it, you see we Grenadiers were long gone by then... would you like to know what actually happened during those early battles Captain, how we managed to transform a lush green landscape into the cradling nightmare that keeps the Gin flowing to this very day...It was the orchestration, the ordered numbers and the arrogance of old men. My boys, my everything, faith, honour and strong together, we were ready...thirty-nine lives in the 1st Battalion charge, I wasn't afraid, I had a good horse and I was angry, we advanced further than we ever dreamed, breaking through the German machines. A few got picked off but none of my boys, the 2nd charge and then the 3rd, the 3rd we got it bad, really bad, lost all I hold dear in a hand full of seconds and as for m-e-e-e...I was shall we say 'passing', full of holes, a bag of broken bones, I couldn't move let alone fight, I was no use to anyone...and do you know what my superiors did Mr. Lidman, do'ya kno-o-ow...they tied me to the saddle with sandbag rope...and sent me off with the 4th anyway, just for the hell of it, right into the guns, the big ones...some... somebody fou-u-nd me, wrapped in a grave of barbed wire and river rest, two days after the charge, with all sorts hanging out. How I was still alive is just...unthinkable, maybe I was angry then too.

The soldiers that took the time, the time to dig me up, cut me out and cart me off on a stretcher were not of my camp or rank, they weren't even from the same army, they were Australians for god's sake!...I was frightened, cold and fading away, I remember a tent, the rattling wind and khaki coloured sheets, I remember the screams, the pungent smell and yes Mr. Lidman I remember 'her', vividly, quite apparent she was, the only one who could long tail across days, you see most nurse's after a while would either collapse from exhaustion or get what we used to call the 'Raving Nancy's', a nurse starts jumping up and down making sounds like a rusty gate. This tended to happen to the youngest ones but your wife was not young, was she? At least forty give or take..."

Paddling in near paralysis, a mute Lidman painfully nods. Sorrow, sadness and Mr. Drop, the unearthly names of three dark tears running the ridge of his hairy earlobe.

"Nanna-oh-nanna, haven't thought about her in an age," remarked the darkness. "There was a young man in the bed next to me, a toffee nosed mommy's boy you know the type, he had the smallest shrapnel cut along his knee, crying like a pitiful child, she bandaged him up and then unraveled that rhyme for him, made everyone laugh, we liked it...she would never tell us her real name, so Nanna it was, I hold a small urge to know her true handle...but I have a feeling it would pale my opinion of her..."

"She...died of typhus," said the sooted corner.

"Typhus was it? I heard something of the like... bet she put up a fight, a remarkable constitution for a woman...I would watch her whirl amongst an army of new wounded, how fast she moved, the energy, like a daddy long legs making its way up a wall, she had this profound hatred of death like a tar taste growing stronger, she kept us alive with her ways, 'ya'gunna live our'boy, ya'gunna live long', she would keep you talking about home, slap you hard around the face, anything to stop you passing, most Nurses would have let me go, 'bring in the next Lad, this ones bought it'...but not her, she would just keep grabbing you and slapping you and throwing the other Nurses around, hell she even gave me some of her own blood Mr. Lidman, 'ya'gunna li-i-ive our'boy, ya'gunna live long'...the first and last thing she ever said to me..."

Confusing shadows swaying in his peripheral, Lidman tries to pin the exact position of the Greeks horrid hisses in the obsidian bliss, a candleless coop.

"The mass of life she must have saved, all those years ago. I've never been a gambling man, a senseless endeavour, but if one had to, a forced flutter on someone, anyone saving a life beyond their own, I'd place every blood covered penny I have on that nelly Nurse....you've made it to five Mr. Lidman, the first ever to do so...and in effect of such rarities...I'll be leaving."

Settled in a paralysed state, DL's light blind bulbs dart around the ceiling, his confusion expressed in a fit of wimpish mumbles.

"...There is a sad but solid system for maintaining my sanity," said a passing shadow.

"Gathering five flaws to justify taking a life needs to be fair for the air of righteousness, five virtues and they're free, very selective obviously, like a terrible game they don't even know they're playing, your cleverness, your kindness, the love you have for your child, a flash of honour and right at the last Captain, unexpected, your exquisite taste in women…"

The tinkling clink of grey glass being reclipped, chimes by the threshold.

"What a night, a well deserved lily…or maybe two…or even four…"

Treading tiles in the prick eared silence, soft sporadic tones dissipate into the distance. A lulling Lidman, growing sleepy, bulbs rolling back, consciousness swaying in and out like little waves stretching their length along a pearly white shore, washing his perspective of minutes into seconds slowly forming to a melon shaped hour, half blinks, little breaths, bedded in period weaves.

Jolting awake, loud cracks of disorientation, gasping, shivering, his lacking lungs filled with a big balloon of frigid air, sharp to a sore throat as high frequencies of bright alabaster rain painfully to the back of his rod cone arrangement, the cottage lights are back on. In a moment of mortal flinching he rolls on to a squealing shoulder, scan darting the colourful bunt in a dazed panic, the surviving stamp of the morning dawn parades its grey blue haze through the heavy oak entrance, left wide open for the chill, an arctic bliss, his teeth chattering with great vapour.

Ogling a chair of cold leather, kin relief, the gentle up and down chest of Marian's goose pimpled body, peaceful, sedate, alive. Upon validating the ginger warmth still emanating from a crusted cold sore, Lidman weakly clasps the banister frame, hoisting up a badly beaten torso, his quivering logs supported by an oddly redeemed strength.

Palming his Yemen flag crackle of dry blood cotton, Daniel advances the freed rail, clogging infant-like over to M. Pulsed by a parental urge to cover her quick, he prepares his old journeying bones to close the source of unwanted chill. Creaking stiff and idle around a cold leather chair front, he reaches out to stroke a daughterly blonde bonce with a ham of hairy knuckles, frowning, something is wrong, fingers are numb, whole arm is numb, turning lifeless by his side, Déjà vu, shocked back to life by vertical rods of searing pain, racing from shoulder to thumb and back again, over and over. Feeling light headed, his new-found lung capacity ages away, breathless, salivating, the taste of copper.

"Oh god, oh no."

Winding elastic, an elderly vice turning tighter and tighter around a choking chest cavity, dragging him down back to the ground in front of Marian's chair, his ocean eyes slam tightly shut, his mouth the complete opposite, clutching his pounding heart with a rattling coiled claw.

And why, why indeed I may ask the same, because it's time Comrades! What patient little particles you are...don't think for one second that I don't feel embarrassed, feel guilty, a neglecting throb am I, all of these things, I do, I do, I have more or less...mostly less, missed out on your entire leading narrative but you will note that I am here at the last with warm kisses and chocolate hugs. Now where is he, I hate to be impatient but where is he...where is my Monkey, oh look he's down there, I'm not no fly I'm footed and fair...well as fair as air can carry me, or maybe I'll drip along the picture frames what a happy hoot... either way I descend with this finishing beginning, I will never forget you my dying Erectus, my brilliant ape, I can't forget you. Now let me drop and get on top, let me tentacleise, a loving incubus on your rocking rack of broken ribs that I may lean in and lick the discoloured skin flakes from your wandering hairline. Yes, I know you're in pain shuuu...try and stay still and relax...you did well Monkey, for a good, good while and changed a great many things, it will all have to go back to normal of course but impressive nonetheless, the time has come to lay with your fossilised features, strike a pretty pose...there's just one last thing to do, I've been growing your eventual irregular rhythm for years, I'm going to grab it hard, comprendo Simio...lay back, enjoy if you can, oh-h-h my that is a fat one, a fat plump pumper, look at it trying so hard to stay in tune... look it missed one...and another...so much pain little ape, let's wind down and around, that's the way hey.

Pounding his dying arms and legs around the red rouge, Daniel wells up with oxygen salt bubbles, counting his seconds in breath length, carefully giving and receiving through a closing oesophagus.

Hmm now that is odd, curious even, I may be a donkey's do-do but I take pride in a punctual stoppage and my clanger is finding it rather hard to stop your tock, it doesn't feel like punny paper, it feels more like plum pudding, something's been pushing it, made it squeal and squawk, yes indeed, who's been working your pump box little Primeo?...I gasp at you, you broke my clanger, this is very disappointing, we're running out of time, you're so tired and old, I don't understand... don't you want to come with me? Don't you want to coil and boil in the oil with me?..I suddenly feel afraid, I don't think I've ever felt afraid before.

Defeating the ready Rain and the Wild Wind, a mighty reverberation of cavalry footsteps charges passed the mud stained mat into a freezing scullery, one cold doctor accompanied by three blue bob-bies, called in the daily dawn by a Brummie po-lice box hissing hymns of Navis lane and torture, a talented teller.

It must not be then...most would have been in my back sack by now, the hands have lapsed so I must leave, you will join me one day won't you little ape...for cuddles.

Jerking left to right in a Siberian chill, Lid-man's fisted throat laxxes in a laying vortex of malodorous air and the care of kneeling uniforms.

You faced so much pain to maintain your exist-ence, you must have a big smile ahead of you, a child's smile no doubt, looky-looky it's true, it's true with acceleration I see you, I see everything, I can touch everything, I even have a card here for you...what lovely handwriting she has...shall I read it to you Monkey, your future...

To Grandad.

The bestest grandad in the whole wide world.

Hope you like the coin book and the tie, mam bought them but I picked them.

Hope I see you soon, love and miss you and have an amazing birthday.

Love Sophie xxx

PS mam and dad say im as stubborn as you. :)

Printed in Poland
by Amazon Fulfillment
Poland Sp. z o.o., Wrocław
01 April 2022

a5f48bb4-2d25-4732-acb4-233363f1a702R02